The Unlikely Promise

A Novel By
Steven Green

*To Matt & Cheryl,
love, [signature]*

authorHOUSE

AuthorHouse™
1663 Liberty Drive, Suite 200
Bloomington, IN 47403
www.authorhouse.com
Phone: 1-800-839-8640

© 2008 Steven Green. All rights reserved.

No part of this book may be reproduced, stored in a retrieval system, or transmitted by any means without the written permission of the author.

First published by AuthorHouse 3/13/2008

ISBN: 978-1-4343-6001-4 (sc)

Printed in the United States of America
Bloomington, Indiana

This book is printed on acid-free paper.

Dedicated to the memory of my wife, Pamela Jean Green without whose encouragement this work would never have been completed.

&

My daughter, Jennifer

Special thanks to Angie Brock Caudle for giving me so much encouragement to continue this labor of love during a difficult time.

Each character in this book is a mixture of many people I have known in my life from the several states in which I have lived. No one character is representative of any factual person.

CHAPTER I
Josh

He rushed downstairs, stuffing his blue oxford cloth shirt into his navy blue pants as he leaped two steps at a time. Running late again. If he had any hope of getting to homeroom on time, Josh would have to forego breakfast again. "My God," his mother said as she heard him. "Sounds like a herd of elephants closing in on us." David Gershwin looked up from his paper and coffee and smiled at his wife. "Well, you know how seventeen-year-old boys are, Lois. Always in a hurry to catch up for the time they spent procrastinating."

"Well, that may be, dear, but Josh's been running late too often these last few weeks. He always used to sit down with us for a bite before going to school. You watch; he's going to come flying in here in a second and tell me he has to have the car today or he'll be—"

"Mom, I gotta have the car today or I'll never make it before school starts."

David chuckled without looking up as Lois eyed her son, not knowing whether to take satisfaction in having been correct or to feel put upon by having to wait until 3:30 to do the errands she had planned.

"Keys are on the counter, Josh, and be home by 3:30, no later."

"Thanks Mom, you're a life-saver. Mrs. Sutton said if I was late again this week, it's the big D, and I just can't take detention again."

"Why don't you try a novel idea, Josh, and get up earlier?" asked his father with a hint of a smile.

If he heard him, Josh didn't respond but frantically grabbed a piece of toast from the table and the keys from the counter; he then bolted out of the kitchen with a "See ya later" tossed over his shoulder.

Out the door he flew and down the sidewalk. Brushes, the basset hound, had leaped from the stoop for safety (no easy task for this breed) as the front door flew open and she eyed her gangly friend as he bounded down the sidewalk and into the car from the passenger's side. Content that the storm of dashing feet was over, she recaptured her spot and slowly lay down again with a long sigh as she heard the car engine start and the tires screech away from the curb. No doubt she was relieved to have anticipated those big feet and gotten quickly (at least for her) out of the way.

Josh's neighborhood was typical of the upper-middle class of Richmond, Virginia, in the mid-1960s; '64 in particular. He liked living in the city, though some of his friends had moved to the suburbs and now attended county schools. Most of the homes in his area were brick, two-story affairs with nice front and back yards. Typical of houses in Richmond then were alleys separating your backyard from the next backyard and house behind you. Josh's was no different, except some had stand-alone garages opening into the alley. His did not.

The weather was overcast and muggy, normal for mid-September. "WLIE, Richmond," the jingle sang as the deejay quickly updated the weather with promises of a humid day and thundershowers by afternoon. The opening chords of "Louie Louie" sounded and normally Josh would have geared up to try again to decipher what the hell that guy from the Kingsmen was saying. The song was almost certainly dirty but you could make so many different words fit no one seemed to have a handle on exactly which parts or acts were in what verses; but everyone, including Congress, seemed to be trying. Supposedly a senator had recommended the investigation be dropped because the song was totally and completely unintelligible! But this morning Josh was preoccupied and just kind of drummed his fingers to the guitar chords and splashy cymbals.

As he drove the two miles or so down Malvern Avenue to school, Josh thought about his almost being late again. He was having a terrible time getting up in the morning and he didn't know why. Maybe it was because he thought school was sort of a drag. He had to remind himself that it was one of those things his dad always told him about "life." The speech went like this: "Uh, son, there are things in this life you've just got to do whether you like it or not and getting an education is one of them." Well, maybe, but the good thing was he'd get to see Penny again. It definitely would be better, he thought, if he could get himself back on schedule again, so he wouldn't have to catch grief from his parents as he flew around the house trying to get ready, shrugging or ignoring questions like the one this morning from his dad about getting up earlier. Sometimes the old shrug was the best way to get out of answering questions from parents. Seems like they just didn't know how to handle a good shrug. Yeah, a shrug might make one look like an idiot but it definitely allowed him to avoid conversations he did not want to have. He had to admit, though, that he was pretty fortunate as his parents did cut him some slack as long as he was doing well with his grades. Until recently that was not a problem, but he was feeling a little overwhelmed lately, which worried him. He quickly looked in the mirror and noticed that he hadn't done much with his dark, wavy hair in his mad rush out. Reaching over into the glove compartment, he found a comb and quickly dragged it through his hair, eyes watering as it snagged twice. *"Ouch,* that hurts!" he said aloud to no one.

Josh was a good-looking kid, six feet tall at seventeen, with dark hair, freckles, and blue eyes. He wasn't clumsy, exactly—just lanky. He got in his own way part of the time. You might say he was sort of "growing into his feet," which were size twelve! A senior at Thomas Jefferson High School, he was interested in the usual teenage things—including sports, but really as a spectator, which was fine with his mother. She was convinced that if you had to be interested in athletics, then you should watch the game from the stands and keep your teeth and bones safe. He wasn't afraid of getting hurt; he just didn't have any real natural talent.

He began to cross Monument Ave., only a block or so from school. Known as one of the more beautiful streets in any city, Monument Ave. boasted numerous statues of Confederate heroes, including Robert E. Lee and Stonewall Jackson, a few miles east of the school. He never really paid much attention to them in the past, but lately he found himself eyeing these bronze figures on horseback whenever he road past them. Hard to believe that these guys actually lived a hundred years ago and did all the things for which the history books gave them credit.

Until recently he'd never really given the Civil War or Richmond's role in it, as capital of the Confederacy, much thought. Suddenly he felt a little light-headed and a chill overtook him. Ever since his dad had bought an 1863 antique Springfield rifle at a collector's auction, his interest in "the rebellion" had grown and he'd begun reading about the war. The latest epic to capture his fancy was *The Lost Cause*—speaking of which, that is exactly what he was going to be, he realized as he shook his head clear, if he didn't hurry. He grabbed a parking spot just vacated by a parent that dropped off her kid. What luck! He pulled in quickly but carefully to the space and dashed, balancing his books, down the block and up the steep steps into the high school.

Thomas Jefferson High School, or "TJ" as it was called by the students, was undergoing changes reflective of Richmond. It was losing some of its upper-middle class students, including most of Josh's friends, to the steadily growing county suburbs; the once-intense rivalry between it and John Marshall High School, where Josh's dad went, was mostly a thing of the past. New rivalries were springing up with Freeman High and the newer Tucker High School, both in fashionable Henrico county. Still, the old school really looked the part, with its mushroom-color facade and grand steps up the front. It was full of character, in contrast to the modern "architecture" of the 60's schools with their silly-looking, aluminum- covered walkways supported by a bunch of spindly poles.

Once in the yellow brick and marble halls, Josh raced up the stairs and bounded into his homeroom and into his desk without a minute to spare. Mrs. Sutton looked at Josh and then at the clock on the wall as it clicked to the start of the school day. He liked Mrs. Sutton and thought she was actually kind of attractive, considering she was probably thirty-three or four. She had a sort of southern belle look with long, dark hair, dark eyes, and a nice figure. But lately she was on his case and he was determined to stay out of her way today, having started with a shaky entrance.

"Hi Penny," Josh said a little sheepishly to the girl who sat next to him in homeroom this year. *God she's cute,* he thought for the thousandth time as he stared at her long, wavy brown hair and dark brown eyes. Her smile was a killer and she knew it. She had almond eyes and great cheekbones that just made her face a perfect shape. They had chemistry between them, no doubt about it. At least from his perspective, anyway. Not even a month into the school year and already he knew that this girl was special. She was new to Richmond.

No one knew much about her except that she moved here with her parents and brother from the western part of the state. Of course, Josh was going to have to figure out how to actually converse with her eventually and perhaps even say something intelligent!

One would think that a good looking, reasonably confident, and savvy kid could at least manage a few more words in a month than "hi!" Once, she actually spoke to him, asking him, "How are you today, Josh?" In his suave and totally classy way he responded, "Uh...I, um, are....fine." He remembered the burning ears and blushing cheeks after that bout: In one fell swoop he had destroyed his cool image and sounded like the southern geek which he tried so hard to avoid.

Well, today would be different: He would walk with her to English, one of the two classes that they shared, and he would very calmly and coolly strike up a real conversation. Then later, on the way to history, their final class, he would just mention Sam's party Saturday night and ask her smoothly if she would like to go with him.

Josh's daydreaming was interrupted by the PA announcements over the loudspeaker that hung on the wall at the front of the class. It reminded him of one of those old-fashioned wooden radios that appeared now and then—the kind over which one always expected to hear the crackly broadcast of the attack on Pearl Harbor at every sighting.

First, there was the ritual of someone in the office turning on the microphone too soon, resulting in everyone hearing papers shuffling, a chair moving, and the principle clearing his throat as he whispered, "Is it on?" Next came the usual announcements that would bore everyone to tears. And finally, the first bell would sound. After this morning's announcements, Josh stood up, watching Penny out of the corner of his eye so as to not be obvious, but also to not lose sight of her. She smiled a knowing smile to herself as she glided into her aisle, and he made a quick move into his to catch up to her.

Of course, it would have been better had he looked first. Then he might have seen Mrs. Sutton approaching his desk to discuss his almost being late again. To his horror, his arm hit his teacher's breasts and his lips bumped her nose as he plowed into her, knocking her backwards across the aisle and into Jimmy Rolfe's newly vacated seat. To make matters worse, he tried to minimize the collision by shifting his weight to his left, whereupon he immediately lost his balance and his books and tripped over the desk. The last thing he remembered was Penny's look of astonishment as he disappeared below desktop level on his way to the floor.

The laughter had finally died down as everyone had hurried out of homeroom to make his or her first class (or to escape the humiliation). Josh lay on the floor for a minute, trying to figure how to shrink himself into one of those little dust balls that caught his eye under the desk. He lifted his head partly to see if Mrs. Sutton was all right and to make sure she wasn't about to hit him with some blunt object. She was sort of half-sitting, half-lying in Jimmy's seat, attempting to get herself together and stand up. *Well, she does have nice legs*, Josh thought as he saw more of them than he should have as she tried to get back on her feet. Only a male teenager in the midst of such horror could have at that split-second thought about sex while trying to figure how to escape from sheer embarrassment and humiliation ... not to mention the dire straits he was surely now in.

"Oh shit, Mrs. Sutton. I'm sorry," Josh said, realizing instantly from the added surprise in her eyes that he had just made matters worse. *Damn, the terrible burden of being a teenager and having two sets of languages to use. One, "Oh gee," for adults and the other, "Oh shit," for your friends. When things got out of hand you never knew which language was going to come flying out.* Things had definitely gotten out of hand here and his brain was just not working as fast as his adrenaline.

CHAPTER II
The Big D

It was late and the muggy, cloudy day hid the usual shadows that were cast in late afternoon on the eastern side of the school where Josh now sat in detention at 4:00 p.m. *Christ, I'm in trouble now,* Josh thought. *Mom expected me home by 3:30 and here I sit.* As his thoughts backed up to the eventful moment this morning, he felt sorry for himself. This day had definitely not turned out to his liking…that was an understatement. *Life just stinks sometimes is all. Mrs. Sutton sure has great legs, though.* He found himself wondering what Penny's legs looked like.

His dream of asking Penny to the party did not come true, to put it mildly. After the debacle in homeroom, Penny refused to acknowledge his presence the rest of the day. Even his usual "hi's" got only a slightly better than icy stare on the way to and from English and history. It was obvious; she didn't want anyone to even *think* she knew such a square! However, he did perceive what he thought was Penny trying to hide a smile when he waved to her after the last bell, but he couldn't be sure it had anything to do with him.

Christ! I am a square! Here I am sitting in detention thinking about her. Get a grip. My God! If it wasn't for her, I wouldn't be in here. Good try Josh, he thought, but he couldn't push her from his mind.

Mrs. Sutton had not been very understanding once he'd helped her to her feet. He had apologized, using his absolute best manners, and while she had softened somewhat, she was certain that his almost being late again had precipitated her winding up in a less than dignified sprawl in the chair. Throw in the *"oh, shit"* and there was no escaping the Big D. It could have been worse, he figured, if she'd sent him to see Mr. Ivers, the principal. Josh didn't fear the principal's wrath, just his lectures. *Damn, that guy was successful in making the whole school behave just to avoid hearing those lectures. Somehow that didn't seem to be playing fair. Of course, who said school principals have to play fair anyway!*

He sat there all alone in the old classroom with its wooden trim, real blackboards (as opposed to the green blackboards in the newer schools), and one-piece desks—those goofy things that were not made for human beings. They made a student feel as though he were in a cramped soapbox derby car. Josh dozed ever so slightly and then woke abruptly with a start after only a few minutes had passed. He had been dreaming. He didn't remember it all, but he recalled standing in front of the statue of Robert E. Lee on Lee Circle and Monument Avenue but Traveler's saddle was empty. Lee was gone! Weird! Suddenly the click of the clock as the hand jumped brought him back to reality. It was 4:30 and time to go. He was on his honor to stay until 4:30 and after the lousy events of this day, he wasn't taking any chances in leaving even one minute early.

As he drove home, his mind wandered back and forth between that weird dream and Penny's beautiful face. *Damn! The high cheekbones, soft mouth, and deep-set brown eyes under those sexy eyebrows were almost haunting.* It was her whole persona and she knew it. Maybe that's what really got to him: the fact that he was convinced she knew it and was able to manipulate him if she wanted to. *What the hell, she doesn't need to.* He was doing an outstanding job of manipulating himself into a fool!

He pulled up in front of his house and bounded out of the car and up the walk. Brushes, tail wagging, sighed her usual sigh as she quickly fled out of harm's way as Josh leaped the steps on the porch, tripped on the top one, and then caught himself against the aluminum storm door with a huge rattle and bang. The racket brought Josh's mom running. "Is that you Josh?" she asked, then added under her breath, " as if anyone else makes entrances like that. Where have you been? I told you I needed to run some errands this afternoon. Now most of the places will be closed." She saw the guilty look and guessed. "Oh, don't tell me you were in detention?"

"I'm innocent mom," he replied.

"Yes, I'm sure you are, Josh," she said with a sarcastic sigh. "What happened?"

"Well," Josh started and he filled her in but decided to leave out a few minor details, like why he had tripped, Ms. Sutton's great legs, and, oh yeah, the bad language part, too.

"Josh, she wouldn't give you detention for simply tripping unless there was more to it, like maybe she felt you did it to clown around and show off?"

"Believe me mom, as stupid as I looked I wouldn't do it to show off."

Lois shook her head and sighed. "Well, Josh, I think you need to spend the afternoon in your room thinking about how you can best avoid detention in the future and get home when you're supposed to."

That works, Josh thought. That's where he was headed anyway, so no sense arguing. He looked appropriately guilty and went up the steps. He caught site of the charcoal portraits of his two sisters and himself on the wall in the living room as he climbed the steps to his room. He missed them. And he missed the family that used to be together as they would gather around the table for breakfast and dinner. Both sisters were married and on their own now. They had married nice Jewish boys, as his mother would say, that were college graduates. Josh liked them both. He wasn't sure if his parents were more happy that they had degrees or that they were both Jewish! He decided in his parents' eyes it was probably a toss up.

    As he turned into the hall at the top of the steps to head toward his room, he noticed the Springfield rifle leaning against the door in his parents' room. His dad had been cleaning it up a bit, though Josh thought it looked pretty good considering it was 101 years old. As he started to go past it, he suddenly felt the same light-headedness and chilly sensation that he had felt that morning. He stopped and studied the thing, picking it up carefully and noticing its heavy, solid feel. He had looked at it a number of times but he hadn't really studied it. Now he suddenly found himself staring at it—the dark brown wooden stock with its little scratches and nicks. He wondered where and how they happened. The silvery gray barrel and trigger mechanism that was only slightly discolored in a few places. It had a little chain that hung from the flintlock. The chain was connected to a sort of cap whose purpose he could not fathom. His dad had said it was unusual to find one with the chain still intact. He noticed too, the date (1862), the eagle, and the words *Springfield, US* engraved on the side plate above the trigger housing. Gazing at it steadily, he wondered how such an instrument of death (it could kill a man at three hundred yards if fired by a decent marksman) could look so graceful and peaceful. It actually had a comfortable feel in its balance. He remembered his dad telling him that this rifle was the standard issue for the Union army.

As he started to put it down, he again felt a chill and his eyes focused upon a small pair of shallow scratches that were etched in the side of the stock. Had these occurred as its young owner had dropped it on the run from advancing Confederates? Had it hit the ground as he fell mortally wounded, a bullet piercing his body? As he read the engraved numbers on the shoulder plate at the back of the stock—517 03 862—he began to feel very faint. Josh set the rifle down quickly and tried to turn towards his room, but he slowly went to his knees and suddenly found himself falling forward, helpless.

CHAPTER III
The Rifle

Feeling as if he were adrift in a fog, Josh slowly started to get up; suddenly, he realized he wasn't lying on the carpet in the hall. Instead, he was on damp grass, the smell of which was mixed with something else … like sulfur. He looked around in a panic, given the bombardment of noise: the sound of men and boys yelling, muffled explosions, and baying horses.

What the hell is this, he thought. *Am I dreaming?* He pinched himself and felt the hurt, but the smells and noise didn't go away. The sun was warm on his back as he raised himself a little and looked around. *This isn't grass; it looks like grain or wheat or something like that.* It had sort of a musty smell. He looked to his left and he could see probably two hundred yards to the crest of a hill. Boys like himself and men of varying ages all dressed in dark blue coats were lying as he was, amidst the tall and trampled wheat or grain. He felt itchy all over and realized he was wearing wool. *Jesus Christ,* he thought, *what the hell is happening here?* Suddenly the breeze died down and white sulfurous smoke hung in pockets all around, swirling over him and blotting out the hot sun until he couldn't see anything. As his sense of panic intensified, everything quieted down in an instant. As quickly as the scene had engulfed him, it vanished. He found himself sitting in the hall again upstairs in his house, dazed, and with the rifle leaning on his knee. With a sigh of relief, Josh slumped down in a heap; little beads of sweat glistened on his forehead. *My God,* he thought, *was that a dream? It seemed so real.* He thought that he could still smell the sulfur from the gunpowder. He suddenly realized the rifle was still touching him and he quickly tossed it onto his parents' bed without looking at it. Shakily, he ambled down the hall to his bedroom, where he collapsed on his bed and slept for an hour.

When Josh awoke, he didn't think about his wild dream or whatever it was. The shadows that began to creep up his pale-blue bedroom wall reminded him that it was almost fall in Virginia, and that reminded him of school, homework, and the events of the day, which depressed him. *What a disastrous day for my love life....as if I had one.* He sulked. He lay there thinking of her—the way she smelled like powder and perfume, the shine in her long wavy hair, and the twinkle in her eyes. He had to admit he wasn't sure he'd seen that twinkle aimed at him *yet.* As he pictured her, his self confidence grew, bolstered for absolutely no logical reason (as if a teenager really needs one) and he was suddenly working up his nerve to call her and ask her to Sam's party. He went to the top of the stairs and heard his mother in the kitchen, cooking dinner. He quickly eased his way into her and his father's room, purposely avoiding the rifle, and he quietly sat on the far side of the bed.

He picked up the phone and dialed Penny's number, so nervous that his fingers stumbled and tripped as he found the numbered holes in the dialer. Then he waited, palms moist, a little short of breath. *Damn, get a hold of yourself, kid; this isn't like you,* he thought. Just then she answered and he realized he hadn't thought of how he would start off the conversation, at which point he tried to say about three things at once, resulting in his accidental biting of his tongue—hard! "Oh God"! He slammed down the phone after having mumbled something even he didn't understand.

Penny stood with the phone still at her ear and tried to replay in her mind what it was she had heard but all she could remember was something to the effect of "Ha..penar..beet...ughaaagggh!" But as she set the heavy black receiver down in its cradle, she smiled faintly.

All through dinner, Josh's ears burned and he played with his food. His dad tried to draw him into a conversation about school. When that failed he even brought up the lyrics to the song "Louie Louie" by the Kinksmen. "That's the Kingsmen, Dad, and no one has a clue what they're saying," Josh announced, not telling the whole truth. In fact, there was a sheet going around school that had the words printed out, which seemed to fit what they were singing, but it all seemed too outlandish to be real. "At night in bed, I..." At any rate, this subject was certainly not something he was going to discuss at dinner with dear mother and father.

"Could I be excused?" Josh asked. "I have a headache and need to finish my homework that I started this afternoon."

He climbed the steps, congratulating himself on escaping the dinner table without having to get into any of the day's misadventures. He considered calling Penny again, but as he felt the little blister on his tongue he thought better of it. Enough disasters for one day. He found his books and actually did finish his homework. As he finally got into bed and closed his eyes, in a fitful sleep he saw himself wearing a dark blue uniform and standing in front of Penny, who was dressed in a green satin period dress with a tiny waist that accentuated her hips. She was crying and hugging him, saying goodbye like a scene from *Gone With the Wind* or something! Then suddenly she vanished and he found himself hugging the ground amidst smoke, explosions, and men shouting.

He felt something under his chest and noticed that he was lying on something hard. He lifted himself and realized that it was a rifle. He quickly grabbed it and looked at the shoulder plate on the end of the stock: 517 03 8622. *Oh my God, this can't be happening*! He jumped up in a panic and suddenly he heard a roar. It sounded as if someone had poured a ton of coins on a tin roof. He realized it was the sound of muskets firing, hundreds of them. Just then someone knocked him down hard, shouting.

"Goddamnit, boy! You tryin' to get yerself and us all heer killed? What unit you from anyway, boy? You one of them stragglers?"

Josh whirled around to see a man, probably in his thirties, crawling away while muttering and shaking his head. He had big sergeant stripes on his shoulder; a short, stocky fellow, he had a wild black beard and mustache with very thick sideburns, like a character out of a movie. But this wasn't any movie and he could hear the sound of minet balls and bullets pinging and ricocheting off everything in sight. *Jesus, this is a time to either wake up from this terrible nightmare or run like hell to get out of here.* But he could do neither. Pinching himself over and over until his arm was too sore to do it again, he looked around again wildly. The sergeant was only ten yards or so away and kept eyeing him every few minutes, so he certainly couldn't jump up again, not without being knocked silly by that sergeant or being shot.

Josh lay still and tried to control his panic. His stomach was churning so badly that he thought he might lose control right there. His body trembled and sweat poured from his face and neck. *What was happening?* His dad always told him that no matter the crisis, stay calm so he could think. Just take deep breaths, slowly exhale each time, and calm would come. *Shit, this is probably a bit more than even Dad would have anticipated,* but he tried it. He breathed slowly over and over again until he'd done it ten times and he did begin to calm down; the panic subsided a bit.

Then he heard a horrifying sound: almost a half-shout, half-animal scream. It grew louder. Josh's spine locked in fear as though he was in a vise, or he no doubt would have sprang to his feet to run, sergeant and bullets be damned. The sergeant himself was on his feet, shouting: "Here they come! Form a line of skirmishers. Get up, men! You won't disappoint old Sergeant Pelter today. We're the best damn sharpshooters this old army's got."

Josh heard that and thought, *If they're counting on me for sharp shooting, then this old army is in real trouble.* Suddenly the sergeant was knocked flat on his back, as though he'd been kicked by a horse. He was motionless. "Oh God, he's been shot!" Josh heard himself shout.

Now the men and boys, lying a matter of yards in all directions from him, jumped up and began to holler in fear. "Let's go! We're doomed!" Another shouted, "Pelter is down; let's get out of here!" As if by order, slowly, tentatively at first, then more quickly, everyone began to get up and move backwards.

Josh somehow managed to force his limbs to work and he jumped up with the rest of them. As he did, he saw an unbelievable sight in front of him: a line of advancing gray-clad men, all yelling at the tops of their lungs. They looked like walking scarecrows. Josh felt that wild yell hit his lower spine and then, like a shock wave, spread out all over his body. The soldiers were coming right at him, elbow to elbow. Less than two hundred yards, Josh guessed. It looked like hundreds and hundreds of men were advancing towards him, perhaps thousands. It didn't matter; he had to get out of there. He realized he was being left behind as his "comrades" retreated—first walking, then trotting, and then finally breaking into a full run for the woods.

Josh skipped the walk and the trot and went full boar into the run. As he ran by the sergeant, Josh's head swiveled on instinct. The grizzled man lie still. Just as he'd fallen, his eyes were staring up at the blue, hazy sky. The front of his navy-blue shirt was discolored and glistening. An increasing puddle of red stained the ground along his sides. *Somewhere, someone had probably just lost a daddy or brother … Shit…* Josh fought off a wave of nausea and continued to run, gripping the rifle as though he would die if he let go of it.

He was in a field of sorts, running and hopping over tall grass or wheat, most of which had been trampled or cut. It was hard to say. He suddenly tripped and fell forward, dropping his rifle. He tried to get up and as he did was hit from behind by a young man, who was running wildly and crying out something hysterically. Josh got up again and saw that he had tripped over a body, one of the scarecrow-looking Rebels,. Wondering how the man had advanced this far, but not stopping to figure it, out he began to run again. Now he could hear something hitting the wheat stalks around him. The stalks were literally flying and bursting apart. "God! Bullets!" he yelled at the top of his lungs. He could hear that sound again of the muskets firing *en masse. Oh God, please be a dream; please wake me up.*

Josh tried to decide who to follow. Hundreds of Union soldiers dressed in dark blue were spread out around him running in a zig-zag manner, dodging the stalks of wheat, and jumping over the slightly trampled ones. Every now and then a man would cry out, fall, and not get up. *Jesus, they're actually getting shot! God, if this is one of your little pranks this would be a really good time to end it.* But there was no end.

He wanted to cry, and in fact realized he *was* crying; tears streamed down his cheeks. *Shit!*

Was he going to die here, in this dream or whatever it was? Could he die here? He tried hard to catch his breath. *I'm only seventeen, goddamnit. I'm not going to die here, wherever here is.* He spotted some woods coming up on his right and he veered off towards them, along with most of the boys around him. Within five feet of the tree line at the edge of the field, he dove with his rifle in hand and quickly crawled behind a tree as soon as he landed. He lay there, panting, trying to catch his breath along with many others in blue.

Suddenly he heard a whistling sound followed by a heavy dull boom in the distance. That was followed by the roar of explosions, of flame and smoke not far from where he lay. As the shabby-looking Rebels came within a hundred yards or so of where he crouched behind a tree, the explosions intensified. The ground shook and he stared as Rebels were tossed into the air amidst the smoke, fire, and dirt and then collapsed to the ground still or rolling.

The Rebels continued to press on and they ran right by him, hundreds of them, pausing to fire ahead, shouting that horrible Rebel yell and trying to dodge what was almost certainly Union artillery fire. The smoke began to drift all around, obscuring everything from time to time until a breeze cleared some of it out again. As he tried to breathe without choking from the sunny haze, Josh could see that something was happening, something shocking. The Union artillery was now taking its toll. The Rebel line was being shredded in the swirling wheat and smoke. Ten or a dozen men crumbled at a time, as if they were leaves being ripped by hail.

In history, Josh had learned about grapeshot-balls of steel in a can dropped into the open muzzle of a canon. When the canon's gunpowder charge was fired, the can disintegrated and the balls, the size of jaw breakers, roared out of the canon barrel like giant shotgun pellets. But that was in a textbook; he didn't expect to see it live! Terrified, he now saw the famous grapeshot in action. *Jesus!* He thought he was going to be sick. But somehow in the midst of all his panic, he was actually watching this incredible scene as though in a movie; his eyes were half open. He was so grateful to be lying in the woods and out of the line of fire that he began to calm down a bit.

As he stared, the Rebels began to move backwards; the onslaught of the artillery and the grapeshot as well as bullets having taken their toll. Someone behind him shouted: "Give 'em hell, boys; fire into their flanks!" With that, the dark green and brown woods suddenly began to come alive with dark blue movement. Union soldiers stood up from their crouched and prone positions and began to load and fire from behind the trees where Josh hid. There was a roar of canon and muskets with the thud of bullets hitting the Southerners. Union reinforcements of some sort were arriving, too. Suddenly, a hail of bullets from the left woods assailed the Rebels from their flank, and they panicked. The infamous Rebel yell turned into muffled shouts of fear as the hunter became the hunted. As the Rebels began backing up and then turning and running, shouts of "kill the bastards" rang out from the woods. Out of nowhere a Union cavalry officer appeared in front of the troops and shouted, "Let's go boys, let's go! Up and after 'em! For all that you hold dear in life, get after them! Today we take the victory with honor!"

Josh, numb at this point, didn't move. He was not opposed to chivalry per se, but he wasn't all that interested in winning the field or any honor; he wasn't looking to have one of those minet balls pierce a body part either. Collecting his thoughts as best as he could, he heard himself say, "Bullshit! No one in his right mind is going after those crazy people. I sure as hell am not."

With that, he turned away from the officer who was some fifty feet in front of him and looked behind him in the woods, noticing for the first time the deep shadows cast by pine and oak. A steady stream of young men were now filing past him out of the shadows, staggering as they came. Some had fearful looks in their eyes, some burned with anger, and still others sported a glazed look that defied explaining but probably mirrored Josh's own look as well. Many of these men were not much older than Josh, if at all. Most had faces streaked with gunpowder, dirt, sweat, and some with tears and blood. But they were all focused on the officer who was yelling at them and to a man, the woods emptied as they formed a line and began pursuing the Rebels in an orderly fashion.

Josh silently stepped back behind his tree and listened to the sound of metal cups, bayonets, and canteens clanging as they trotted towards their enemy. They moved quickly as they followed their lieutenant or whatever he was. Josh waited for what seemed an eternity, trying desperately not to panic and to figure out what he would do next. How would he get out of this? What is this anyway? Is he in a time warp? As the terrible racket ebbed away and his ears began to adjust to the quiet, he heard a new sound coming from the twisted human wreckage that consisted mostly of Rebels that lay in front of him. The soldiers began to moan and cry out.

"Water! Please, God, someone get me water!"

"Julie, oh Jesus, Julie help me, please! It hurts, oh God"!

A new wave of panic washed over Josh. What should he do now? Was this for real—could he really do something to help someone? *Like what? I'm not certainly going to find a Coke machine out here!* Then he spotted a canteen lying ten feet or so in front of him (the one he had was empty). Slowly, without really thinking, he stepped out of the edge of the woods and picked up the canteen. Not focusing on who was on whose side, he just forced himself to walk to the closest body that cried out.

He was a blonde Union soldier lying on his back in the trampled wheat, who was wounded in the left leg just above the knee. Maybe it looked worse than it really was but it looked horrible. The soldier moaned softly, "Please save me, friend." The hot September sun (it must have been mid- afternoon based on its position) burned down through the smoky haze. Josh approached the soldier slowly and thought he would get sick for sure but somehow he managed to lower himself, using the rifle to steady his trembling limbs. He did not look directly at the wound. He opened the cork on the canteen and poured some water into the young man's open mouth.

As he tried to get enough courage to say something, a movement caught Josh's eye to his left. As he looked quickly, he saw a skinny, wounded Rebel—dressed in what looked like tan rags—only a yard from him and coming at him with a musket cradled in his hands.

Before Josh could make a move, the musket was swinging through the air; while he managed to shift his weight slightly, the rifle stock hit him a glancing blow. As though in slow motion, Josh felt an incredible force hit him like nothing he'd ever experienced, not even when he'd been hit by a "slung" bat in baseball practice. Then there was darkness, total darkness.

CHAPTER IV
Answers

Josh could feel his senses returning. He was afraid to open his eyes but then he felt what he hoped was his mattress against his cheek. He slowly opened his eyes to find with great relief that he was lying in his very own bed.. He tried to sit up but felt a terrible pain in his right temple. With all that thrashing around he must have hit his head on the headboard. He could hear voices calling to him from his parents' bedroom, "Josh, are you all right?"

Trying to collect his thoughts, he weakly hollered that he was fine; he had merely tripped coming back from the bathroom. With that thought, he quickly checked to see if he had wet the bed. He hadn't, though it wouldn't have surprised him one bit if he had, as scared as he'd been. *What the shit was going on...what had happened? Was that a dream? What else could it have been?* Still, going over the "dream" in his mind, he wondered how he could picture such vivid scenes of things about which he knew very little. Looking at the clock radio on the nightstand, he was stunned to see that only a couple of hours had elapsed since he had turned out the light to go to bed. *Amazing,* he thought. Fearful of experiencing a similar vision if he fell back asleep, Josh wondered if it were possible for him to not return alive. He lay back down to ponder this bizarre episode, but, exhausted, he fell asleep in minutes.

At 6:30 his alarm rang; instead of the usual reaching over to hit the snooze button, he instantly sat up in bed and turned the light on, making sure that he knew where he was. *Thank God, it's my own bed; no grass, no bodies, no smoke.* Then reaching up to touch his temple, he winced in pain as he felt some swelling.

He walked over and looked in the mirror and could see a bluish-purple bruise over his eye. *Jeez! Maybe some of Mom's makeup will hide it.*

Hurrying to the bathroom at the end of the hall, he quickly rummaged through his mother's cosmetics supply and found a container with beige cover-up cream. Carefully, he spread some on the bruise, wincing as he touched it. *Not bad. Minimal swelling so far. It looks pretty good,* he thought. As he stood there and looked at himself in the mirror, his mind jumped from the catastrophe of his dream to an even worse catastrophe that he would have to face today—this morning in fact: his call last night to Penny.

He could feel the bump on his tongue where he had bitten it while losing his cool. Perhaps she didn't know who had called her. *I mean, after all... how could she have pieced those shredded words together to figure out that it was me?* He decided to say that if she asked him if he had called, he would deny it, plain and simple. *Christ, tongue bites and rifle butts! The latter was just a bad dream....it had to be.* But the bruise on his temple? *No time to think on it now; I've gotta get dressed.*

After the usual breakfast routines, he was on his way to school again; this time, however, he was driven by his mother since she had to have the car that day. *Shit, what a pain.* But he wasn't about to ride his bike anymore (not cool) and forget the bus. So it was walk, find a ride (too late this morning), or convince his mom to take him.

As she approached the school, Josh had her stop a block away so he could get out of the car unseen. Just as he opened the door to fly out, several girls he knew walked by and in unison all shouted and giggled, "Hi, Mrs. Gershwin! Hey, Josh! How are you both?" Lois started to answer but at the sight of Josh's frantic eyes, thought better of it and waved slightly as she pulled away from the curb the second after Josh leaped from the car. Blushing and straggling behind so he wouldn't have to face the girls, he slowly walked and picked up twigs that were still damp with dew from the grass.

It was a warm, humid morning with a bit of a haze and Josh's mind wandered back to the battlefield again, but at the sight of the concrete structure that was his alma mater, all thoughts focused back on Penny and how he could get through the day. He needed a victory. He needed to do something that would impress her and win her over. And he certainly didn't want to tangle with Mrs. Sutton again. Penny was already in her seat chatting with the other students when Josh walked in the classroom.

Mrs. Sutton was sitting at her desk, reading something. As Josh passed her, she looked over at him and he froze for a minute, but then she smiled; he smiled in return. *Whew! That's a good way to start the day—compared to yesterday anyway. Of course, the morning was young!* He walked directly to his desk and squeezed his long, lanky frame into the thing like a contortionist. Then he cast a sideways glance in Penny's direction, expecting to see her still chatting with her friends. To his amazement, he found himself staring directly into her eyes. *Those eyes…oh shit…those wonderful eyes.* It was just too much for him that early in the morning.

He knew full well that it was the morning after he had made such an idiot of himself. But he was determined to stay cool, and, after all, he had a chance to strike up a real conversation with her as he had been planning yesterday when all hell broke loose. Very carefully and with maximum self confidence, he said, "Well, good morning Penny. How are you doing today?"

"Hello, Josh," she said softly, with a trace of a smile—the smile that killed him every time he saw it. "I'm doing really good, thanks. And you?"

"Oh, I'm doing pretty good considering that it's early yet." *Idiot!* he thundered at himself. *What the hell did that mean; why did I say that?*

"You know, last night I could have sworn—"

She was interrupted by Mrs. Sutton calling the homeroom class to order. Josh wondered if she knew he had called. He just smiled and calmly turned his head towards Mrs. Sutton's voice. She was just telling the class that Mr. Ivers had a few announcements this morning and it might delay classes ten minutes or so and that since the principal hadn't yet arrived, they were waiting. He heard Penny's voice again.

"Josh, last night I got the strangest phone call around six o'clock."

Josh felt moisture spread under his armpits in his shirt. "Oh, really? Well, you, uh, that happens sometimes. What kind of, uh, phone call?" he asked with as much indifference as he could muster.

The irony was not lost on Josh: here she was finally talking to him and he had to pretend to be only moderately interested lest he somehow give it away that he was the idiot who had called. Yet the whole purpose of calling her was to be able to talk to her just like this—like a normal person—and invite her to Sam's party, which was what, he realized, he should be doing this instant. *God, don't just look down; help me here!* he thought.

"Are you okay, Josh? You look a little pale!" she said as her eyes bore directly into his, her lips betraying a trace of a smile.

She is playing with me isn't she? She had to know. She was just tossing the little crumbs out there, waiting for my next brilliant move. How did girls learn to do this so young? How could they, with such small bodies and meek appearances, completely dominate and control someone a foot taller and fifty pounds heavier and stronger? It has to be a conspiracy somehow. Were they taking night classes in the basement of the school? Were their mothers casting spells? Handing them down from generation to generation?

He remembered the lines of suitors who appeared when his sisters were still at home. One after another they crumbled and were left drooling and talking to themselves in malt shops, burger drive-ins, and movie theaters, asking themselves questions that had no answers and gesturing to the god of puberty.

He realized that she had asked him a question and he hadn't answered. It was kind of hanging in the air like the voice balloon in a cartoon, except that would have been better because then he could have looked up and read it. He had forgotten what she asked him. He could ask her to repeat it, but that would be tantamount to admitting that he wasn't listening. *Shit.* He tried to think fast; she was just sort of staring at him.

"Josh, are you sure you're okay?"

Ah, that was the question! "Oh, Penny. Yes, I'm fine; I just didn't sleep well last night. Bad dreams, you know…a little tired is all. So tell me about your call," he said, trying to recover, but thinking instantly what a dumb shit he was to bring that up again.

"Oh, it's nothing. Just that whoever he was, I think he was either very nervous or was gagged in mid-sentence. He actually sounded kind of cute; I sort of wish he had called back."

Having said that, her body slowly turned in her seat; as she turned, her gaze lingered just a second with her eyes fixed on his with a trace of a smile. He was about to scream, *It was me… it was meeeeee*, when she swung her head around and started talking to Sally, who sat on the other side of her desk.

That's it, he thought. *I can't take this!* He managed to take a couple of deep breaths to preclude hyperventilating.

Then the familiar shenanigans overtook the microphone. *Here it comes* Josh thought. *Let's see: yes, one feedback squeal, papers rustling, and, oh yes, finally Mr. Ivers' whisper of "Can I talk now?" Oh save me!*

"Students of Thomas Jefferson, this is your principal. Good morning to you all. I just wanted to let you know that we're going to try something a little different this morning. Rather than have everyone rush off to his or her first class at 8:15, I'm asking that you remain in your homerooms a bit longer and listen to a little narrative."

This sounded less than promising, Josh thought.

"As you certainly know, we are in the midst of a centennial anniversary in southern life, especially here in Virginia. Exactly one hundred years ago, the Civil War raged right under our very noses. No other state in the Union had as many battles or as much blood spilled on its soil during the course of the war. You can't get in your car and drive for twenty minutes in any direction from this spot and not see evidence of that war to this very day. Just twenty miles or so east of here was fought one of the shortest and yet bloodiest battles of the war, Cold Harbor.

"You may know the spot if you've driven down Nine Mile Road in the Sandston area by the airport. Not too far from there occurred another lesser-known battle, Malvern Hill, which was part of the Seven Days Battle series where, with terrible losses, Lee kept the Union troops from reaching our fair city, Richmond, and the White House of the Confederacy, downtown just a few miles from here.

"Well, we are fortunate to have with us today a man whose grandfather died on the field that day at Malvern Hill and who, is himself a well-known expert on that battle, Mr. Jonathan Pelter. I've asked Jonathan, a volunteer who works with the Department of Parks and Services, to speak to us today about that battle and to give us just a flavor of what times were like back then."

Pelter... Pelter why does that name sound so familiar? Josh thought. *Must be a coincidence but it sure has a familiar ring to it... hmmm.* As Jonathan Pelter began to address the student body in their homerooms at "TJ," Josh suddenly found himself feeling light-headed while the images of smoke and gunfire returned to the forefront of his consciousness. He was drifting in and out of present awareness, hearing only bits and pieces of Mr. Pelter's remarks, when he heard him say that witnesses claimed that his grandfather, a sergeant in the Union corps, was attempting to rally his troops when several Rebel bullets literally knocked him off his feet.

"OH MY GOD!" exclaimed Josh as he jumped out of his seat. "Sergeant Pelter! My God! He was my sergeant; I saw him get killed just yesterday! I was there!"

Suddenly, pandemonium began to reign in the classroom. First, Mrs. Sutton jumped to her feet and told Josh in no uncertain terms to be quiet and sit down. But he was out of control and didn't really hear her. He was somewhere else now, or his mind was, as he shouted out, exclaiming that he was ducking and dodging bullets, horses, and bodies. He dropped to one knee as if aiming that rifle of his dad's at the front row of students. His classmates leaped for cover, totally perplexed but enjoying it nonetheless. Josh's mind raced. In fact, at some point he threw himself under Mrs. Sutton's desk to avoid being trampled by a horse. His classmates, roaring with laughter, figured that this had to be one of the greatest stunts anyone had yet pulled in the history of the great Thomas Jefferson High School.

"Josh, you come out from under there this instant!" yelled Mrs. Sutton as she stood off to the side of her desk, obviously with no intention of sitting down at it again with Josh beneath it. He'd seen enough of her in their collision yesterday, she remembered uncomfortably. "If you don't come out of there right now, I'm going to send you to Mr. Ivers' office. In fact, I'm sending you there anyway—*right now!*"

She then swung around to the scene in the room. Most of the girls were looking on in disbelief or cringing while the boys were still laughing and taking shots at poor Josh from behind chairs and desks with their imaginary rifles. As she moved out into the center of the room, leering at each of them, everything began to quiet down and they began to take their seats again—most of them feigning that they might get shot as they tentatively stood up unprotected. Penny just sat in her seat dumbfounded. Josh had practically knocked her on the floor when he leaped out of his seat yelling whatever it was he had been yelling. Having been raised in the southwestern part of the state, she was only slightly familiar with the Civil War, mainly the notorious exploits of General Stonewall Jackson and his division of the Stonewall Brigade in the Shenandoah Valley. However, she had certainly never faced it firsthand, especially in a classroom.

Josh was still sitting under the desk but he had more or less regained his awareness and began to peek around the desk into the room. *This doesn't look good,* he thought.

He was trying to remember what on earth he was doing there. Just then he saw Mrs. Sutton appear around the corner of the desk; her face was flushed and even bore traces of perspiration. She didn't look happy and he was, no doubt, the cause!

"Okay Josh, that's it! I don't know what you think you're doing, but you've disrupted this class for the last time this week. Get your books and take yourself to Mr. Ivers' office."

They could both hear in the background that Mr. Pelter had finished his commentary about Malvern Hill and Mr. Ivers was now thanking everyone for their attention; he further asked that they give some thought to seeing the various areas around Richmond that were steeped in Civil War history. In fact, he liked his own idea so much that he suddenly made it an assignment for all the history classes at "TJ," regardless of grade level.

In two weeks, all students were to turn in a paper to their history teacher about what they learned on their visit to whatever Civil War area they chose to focus on around Richmond. To encourage those who had less of an interest and/or aptitude for such a project, in all his magnanimity Mr. Ivers suggested that papers could be submitted by a pair of students— a sort of team event! Mrs. Sutton shook her head, thinking of all the whining she would hear from the history teachers in the teachers' lounge that afternoon. She could just hear them now. *Who the heck does Ivers think he is, making assignments for us? Is he going to be the one to have to grade those papers? How the heck do we know if they did a good job or not? We don't know the details of all the Civil War history around here!*

Suddenly she remembered what she was supposed to be doing and she glared down at Josh, who was now trying to get out from under the desk.

"Did you hear me, Josh?"

"Yes, Mrs. Sutton," he almost whispered. "Uh, could I talk to you out in the hall for a moment? I think I can explain this little misunderstanding."

"You can explain it to Mr. Ivers. I've got better things to do this morning. I can't think of any reason on earth for what you did here this morning." Actually, she had mixed emotions as she looked at him. He was obviously shaken by the whole thing. He looked flushed and truly worried. Too bad! He should have thought about the consequences before acting out such an idiotic scene.

Josh slowly walked back to his seat, picked up his books, and turned towards the door. His eyes met Penny's as he turned and she quickly averted her glance. But in that split second, she, too, saw something in his face that concerned her. She didn't have the problem of saving face that Mrs. Sutton had so she gazed back at him and gave just the slightest hint of a smile. In the midst of the whispers and the chuckling, Josh found solace in that ray of a smile. He smiled a worried smile and walked a bit haltingly to the door, looking back at Mrs. Sutton once more before leaving. She quickly turned to the blackboard and began erasing the previous day's material. With that "signal," Josh left the classroom, having been tossed out for the first time ever.

CHAPTER V
Penny

As Josh closed the door behind him, Penny sat waiting for the first bell, now some 40 minutes late due to the morning's activities. She drummed her fingers on her desk and contemplated her last view of Josh as he had disappeared into the hall with that sad look on his face. She felt some pity for him as she ran her delicate fingers through her long wavy brown hair. and closed her eyes to picture him better.
There was something about Josh. He was tall, good looking and had a sense of humor (that she had not a clue how to figure out but it was there nonetheless). Maybe it was the trace of the little boy still in him and that hint of mischief that made him sexy. He was Jewish, too, and being a Catholic from the southwestern part of the state, she had very little knowledge of Jewish people, having known virtually no Jewish boys. That added to the mystery of this guy. But more than all of that, there was something about him that stirred her inside when he was close. It made her uncomfortable. She was going to keep her distance. No complications or loss of focus. This was her senior year, and she was going to be the first girl in her family to attend college. She was

not going to be dependent on a man for all the things she wanted out of life. She had seen too much of that in her family.

Women taking a secondary role in life! Not that the men in her family had been abusive, far from it, but they had a freedom she envied and that she was determined to have. They had an air about them—as if they had accomplished so much more than their wives or sisters or mothers. And her mother and the others accepted it as just part of the woman's role. That was not going to happen to her.

She knew Josh was interested in her from the start. She could see it, feel it, and her girlfriends said the same thing. She also knew it had to have been Josh who had called the other night so tongue-tied. She had figured that it was his shyness that he had yet to overcome. However, she wasn't about to let her guard down. Still, her thoughts returned to that sad look on his face as he left the room.

Detention is not something that a student wants to have often or try to get used to. The only thing worse than detention, of course, was facing Mr. Ivers. In this case, Josh knew he was in the wrong. Well, not really wrong but he understood the perception of Mrs. Sutton, the class, and how Mr. Ivers was going to react. He might have confided in Mrs. Sutton had she let him explain his odd behavior, but he would never confide to Mr. Ivers.

As he headed for the office, he thought about the events and he didn't understand why he totally lost his awareness in Mrs. Sutton's room. In the other flashback, he had been aware that he was out of place. This time he seemed to be immersed in the role, even trying to fire a rifle. He chalked it up to the sudden realization of hearing Pelter's direct kin speaking. He must have just temporarily flipped out.

As he entered the principal's office, Mr. Ivers was preparing to take Mr. Pelter on a tour of the school (what a thrill that would be, Josh dryly noted). The first bell had rung minutes ago and Ivers was waiting for the halls to clear before venturing out of his safe haven with Pelter. Josh's lucky angel must have been sitting on his shoulder at that moment.

"Mr. Ivers, I have to talk to you about something that happened in Mrs. Sutton's class."

"Where is Mrs. Sutton?" the principle asked as he gave a *what next* look to Mr. Pelter.

"Well, she sent me here to discuss an incident in her homeroom class a few minutes ago."

Mr. Ivers knew Josh was a good student, if prone to a little mischief occasionally. "Did you do anything to hurt anyone or make a sexual remark, Josh?"

"Of course not, Mr. Ivers," Josh replied.

"Well, I am on my way to give Mr. Pelter a tour of the school, so why don't you just think about whatever it is you did for an hour after school today in detention and I will catch up to Mrs. Sutton later to get the details. Does that sound fair?"

Josh was almost beside himself with joy at not having to go through an explanation and then sit through the lecture he had been certain was coming; however, he didn't want to look too happy.

"Yes, Mr. Ivers, that seems fair, considering how busy you are and how much of a misunderstanding this was anyway," Josh said very matter-of-factly.

"Fine, Josh. Let Ms. Applebee know that you are to be in detention today for an hour." With that, Mr. Ivers and his guest hurried out of the office. For once, the timing was perfect. Josh didn't have to go back to Mrs. Sutton's homeroom but could go to his first period bell only a few minutes late, which was now actually his second since first period was replaced with Mr. Pelter. He quickly stepped into the hall and headed for history, the first of the two classes in which he would see Penny that day. The second was English. *History… jeez…* He was reminded of the new assignment the entire school had received today. He would need to think about how he wanted to approach it. With all of the excitement and his trip to the principal's office, he hadn't had much chance to think about Mr. Ivers' little brainstorm. Just then, Sam caught up with him.

"Jesus Christ, Josh, are you losing your mind? What the hell did you pull in homeroom this morning? The whole school is talking about you like you're a loony bird, ass.., or both! What gives?"

Josh thought, *How in hell does word spread that fast in just ten minutes since the bell rang?*

"Depending on who you talk to, you either tried to place Mrs. Sutton under arrest for spying on the Union army, or you tried to destroy General Lee's whole army from behind or under her desk—with very little firepower, I might add! Couldn't you at least have picked the right side to be on?" Sam burst into laughter and gestured as though he was trying to load a rifle with a ramrod.

Sam was Josh's best friend, or he used to be until this moment. They grew up together since childhood and lived only a few blocks away from each other, which was a very convenient thing before they got to the age of driving permits, when bikes and feet were the main mode of travel. Sam was a sharp kid: a little cocky, but heady nevertheless. He was more outgoing than Josh and didn't have the same problem of shyness. He was good with the girls and exuded the confidence in himself that Josh lacked. He was also Jewish. He had dark hair, and had dark eyes framed by a face that was a European and Mediterranean mix. Josh, fair-skinned as he was, looked more European. Together they complimented each other. Sam was reasonably certain he wanted to be a psychiatrist, which, at that moment, Josh thought might be good, since at this rate he was beginning to think he was going to be Sam's first patient.

Josh had not confided in Sam that he was somehow being transported back a hundred years in time at a moment's notice. He didn't think his friend would really understand or appreciate his dilemma and might think he was nuts.

"Shit, Sam, I'll have to explain later; there's no time right now. Just remember that I had my reasons and they were good ones. And by the way, Mrs. Sutton is not spying for the Confederates." With that Josh tapped Sam on the head and left him to hurry to class; turning back to his friend, he tossed out, "She actually works for us by spying on General Lee!" He didn't really feel the humor but it did help ease the tension in him somewhat. Sam looked around quickly, thankful the halls had emptied. "Go to class, you blue-belly northerner."

Josh slowly pushed the door to his history class open and he looked for his seat next to Penny, of course. No sooner had he entered the room than did the sounds of rifle fire as only humans can make it and even a rebel yell rang out.

"Okay, okay…knock it off," he said as he headed for his seat. Penny was already in hers and eyed him carefully.

Before he could even say hello to Mr. Poletts, the teacher confronted him with a sort of half-smile and wagging finger. "Okay, Josh, here's the scoop. The Rebel army has not been spotted in these here parts for at least a half an hour, maybe longer. So I don't expect you to lead any charges in this classroom." His smile quickly vanished. "If you do, I won't take any prisoners… if you read me." *Ouch!* Poletts was a jerk under normal circumstances. Having to take that garbage from him now was a bitter pill, but Josh was not about to say anything that would get him in any deeper than he already was.

Impressed with himself Mr. Poletts walked away and Josh, blushing a bit, looked over at Penny and smiled sheepishly.

"Well, Josh, I don't have the slightest idea what all that was about this morning but if it's notoriety you want, you certainly have it."

For the first time that morning, Josh let his guard down and revealed a bit of the turmoil that was inside of him.

"Notoriety is not what I want, Penny. Maybe I could explain it to you sometime. I mean explain what happened this morning, or rather, what caused this morning's, uh, excitement."

She smiled and sort of rolled her eyes. "Well, that would be an interesting conversation, I'm sure." Expecting him to laugh, she was surprised to see that he only smiled slightly and then looked away to the front of the class where Mr. Poletts was beginning to lecture.

Well, excuse me!, she thought. *I'm not the one who tried to end the southern rebellion in homeroom! Once again, this guy is cute but I'm keeping my distance. Next thing you know, he'll think he's Wyatt Earp and try to throw us all in the lockup!!*

"Okay, class, let's settle down. We probably should talk about your new assignment from this morning, courtesy of Mr. Ivers," Mr. Poletts said. He mumbled something else but Josh couldn't understand it. "Since this is a history class and I will be grading your papers, let's agree that each paper is to be no more than three pages in typed length. Take a few moments and pick a partner with whom you're going to work on this project and then, since you don't have that much time to complete the assignment, why don't you take the first twenty minutes of the period to talk over your plans with your partner."

It suddenly dawned on Josh that this was his chance. He turned to Penny and blurted out, "Penny, would you consider working with me on this project? I know a little about the Civil War." At that moment one of the other students, a big guy named Donald, came up to Penny and asked if she would like to work with him on it. Looking over at Josh, he sneered and said, "That is, unless General Grant over there has already enlisted you into his regiment."

"Very funny, Don," Josh retorted.

Penny just eyed them both. " What are you doing your reports on?"

Don answered, "The Chimberazzo Hospital over towards the airport. The hospital isn't standing anymore but the Richmond Battlefield Headquarters is on the same site and has lots of info and pictures." Penny looked over at Josh and waited for him to answer. He was looking down at his shoes, deep in thought.

"Josh, what are you going to report on? Do you know yet?"

He wanted to say, *yes I know, but it shouldn't matter. You should want to be my partner no matter what!* Not to cut off his nose to spite his face, though, he replied, "Yes, I'm going to do mine on the battle at Malvern Hill." *After all, that's where I fought during the war,* he thought, but said nothing.

"Hmm, I think I'd be more interested in the hospital than the battlefield," Penny said, eyeing Josh for any reaction.

"Great!" said Donald, "I'll call you tonight and we can plan the visit to the site and also when we can get together to start."

Josh turned in his chair to face the other side of the room, his face flushed and his body rigid. Donald ambled back to his seat totally impressed with himself.

Penny felt a little sorry now, but it wasn't her fault that Donald had a more interesting topic and she certainly didn't owe Josh anything. Was that really it? Or was she just keeping her promise to herself? *Steer clear of complications.* Still, she wondered if she had made a mistake.

That night after dinner, Penny sat in the big overstuffed chair in the living room of their smallish red-brick ranch house and waited for Donald to call. She didn't feel any attraction to him whatsoever.

He was safe. She could do this project and not give a thought about anything but getting a good grade, which she could use, because history was not one of her best classes. She was hovering between a *C* and a *B*. She wanted to go to the University of Virginia and it would definitely require above-average grades to get there. She was trying to convince herself that she had made the right decision and she knew it. She could still see the hurt that Josh tried to hide.

Just then the phone rang and she waited while her mother answered. Silence. "Penny, it's for you. It's… a.. Donald."

"Thanks, Mom," she said, coming to the kitchen to get the phone; it was the only one in the house besides the one in her parents' bedroom. She waited to see if her mom would leave, but she was busy cleaning the kitchen so Penny stretched the cord around the doorway into the dining room.

"Hello," she said softly.

"Hi, Penny. It's Donald calling you about the project we're doing together. Boy that Josh, what a nerd, huh? I heard what he did this morning. Sounds more like a kid than a high school senior. It figures; he's Jewish!"

Penny felt a rush of anger come over her and before she could even think it through, she heard herself say, "Well, Donald, actually Josh is a friend of mine and I don't appreciate your talking about him that way. I think it would be best if you and I did not do our projects together." There was silence for a long, uncomfortable moment.

"If he's such a good friend, then why didn't you just say you would do your project with him to begin with?" Donald asked, obviously a bit hurt and angry.

Penny didn't feel she had to answer that. Without so much as a pause, she calmly and icily said, " Donald, that is really none of your business. I am sorry that this isn't going to work out; I hope you will be able to find another partner for your project."

"Don't worry about me, girl; there's plenty where you came from. You chicks think you can do anything you want, anytime you want. Well, the hell you can! I'm—"

Penny softly put the phone down in its cradle on the wall. She wasn't going to listen to that trash from him. Well, she'd made a mess of this. It really wasn't all Donald's fault. She was sure many of the kids had a grand time at dinner this evening, retelling the story of Josh and his exploits today. *Let's face it, most days when mom or dad asks what happened in school you had virtually nothing to say.* At the same time, it surprised her that she had gotten so angry in defense of Josh. *What was that all about? Maybe it was just a feeling for the underdog or that crack about his being Jewish. Well, what's done is done.* Tomorrow she would have to find another partner for this silly project and move on.

"Anything wrong, dear?" her Mom inquired.

"No, not really, just discussing a project for school," she answered as she walked back to her big chair and picked up her English book to finish the day's assignment. Then for a second, she thought *What if Josh doesn't have a partner yet?*

CHAPTER VI
TGIF

Josh was up early and downstairs in time for breakfast, which made his mother suspicious. He went directly to his usual place at the table in the breakfast room. Several years ago his parents had added a pine paneled den and breakfast room off the kitchen which was too small to eat in. It was Friday and he was anxious to be done with this school week. Yesterday had been another day to forget—total humiliation in class and a rejection by Penny as well. He hadn't said much at dinner or afterwards, in spite of several attempts by his parents to engage him in conversation. Now he just wanted to down a piece of toast and an egg and be off to get this day over with.

"Josh, you were awful quiet last night. Anything bothering you?" his mom asked as she put a plate in front of both him and his dad.

"Well, yesterday wasn't one of my best days—nor was this my best week, for that matter; it's been a real bummer," Josh said in between gulps of orange juice. "But not life threatening, so I'll make it."

"What happened? Something school related, or problems with friends?" his dad asked while buttering a piece of toast.

Josh wasn't going to get into it this morning, but he appreciated his dad's interest.

"Actually, it's kind of personal. I'm just kind of struggling to get through something right now but if I need some advice I'll for sure let you know." That seemed to satisfy them. No more questions.

He had slept uneventfully last night, thank God. No guns, no soldiers, nothing. Maybe this little experience had run its course. He could only hope.

Sam was going to drive this morning so he had to get going. As usual, he would walk the few blocks to Sam's house to meet him. As he bounded down the steps from the porch, Brushes came running from the bushes where he had been dozing.

"Morning, boy; let's go." No other words were necessary. Brushes knew that meant they were walking to Sam's because Josh was going to ride to school with his friend. Josh knew Brushes longed for the days when he used to be able to walk to school with them and then would leisurely amble home by himself or play in the area of the school till they came out in the afternoon and walked home with him. That was a long time ago. Then they changed schools and they rode bikes. He tried following them a few times, running along behind, but with his stubby short legs that just didn't work. Now of course they rode in cars and that scared the bejesus out of the dog. The little sandy-haired cocker down the street got nailed not too long ago. Brushes himself had been hit one morning while Josh and his dad were witnesses. Josh's dad was waiting on the bus and Josh was on his bike leaving for school when he'd made the almost fatal mistake of not looking before dashing across to Josh's dad. It was a miracle but the car's bumper just barely touched him as he rolled up in a ball and none of the wheels hit him as the car passed over him.

The worst part of it was the sound of those damn screeching tires and that awful smell of rubber burning. With his sensitive sense of smell and hearing, the poor animal was sick for two days. Hopefully he wouldn't make that mistake again. But the dog did love the attention and the sympathy that had been lavished on him for a few days.

Sam was already outside as Josh and Brushes rounded the corner.

"Hey, Brushes! What's up, boy?" Sam said as he flipped the dog's big ears up in the air. "Well, Josh, are you going to tell me what really happened yesterday or what?" Sam asked as he went around to the driver's side of the car and slid into the big white Buick. Sam's parents always had a big new car. Josh's dad always bought used cars. Josh had decided when he was an adult he was going to buy new cars. The smell alone was worth it.

"So long, Brushes, hope you get lucky today," joked Josh as he jumped into the car.

Brushes just shook his head and headed back home probably thinking, *yeah as if my "master" was Mr. Lucky himself these days.*

"Not this morning—not enough time to get into the whole story," Josh finally replied. "But I'll tell you one thing: Penny sure did me in yesterday. I was going to do that project of Mr. Ivers' with her, but she picked Donald Jones instead."

"Donald Jones? He's so damn arrogant. I figured you and I would work on that goofy project together, you dummy," Sam said while pulling away from the curb.

"Well, I did, too, until I saw a chance to spend some time with Penny and let her get to know me. You know I've been thinking about her since I first saw her at the beginning of the year."

"Yeah, I know," Sam said. "She's not Jewish. How do you think that would play at home?"

"Shit, I don't know but I'm not going to worry about that now. First things first. I haven't even hardly gotten to know her yet."

"Well, here's another flash for you, after all the shit you pulled this week; I find it hard to believe she'd even let on that she knows you. Schmuck. That's why she chose Donald over you, I'm sure. And another thing, I bet her parents would give her shit if she did agree to go out with you. They're from back in western Virginia, Josh. They still think Jews have horns and bay at the moon out there."

"Listen, Sam," Josh said as serious as he ever got. "All that shit in school this week? There's something going on in my head."

"Boy, I'll say—something like a baseball game with no outfielders?" Sam joked as he pushed hard on the accelerator and flew across the busy intersection of Patterson and Malvern Avenues. Malvern was a typical wide, pretty street in this part of Richmond, lined with older trees and big homes of many types of architecture.

They were only a few blocks from school so Josh wasn't about to divulge the gory details. "Well, you can laugh but all I can tell you for now is I've had some flashbacks."

"Flashbacks!" Sam yelped. "Shit, I used to walk in my sleep. Flashbacks are just normal tricks that your head plays on you. You know, replaying events in your sleep that your subconscious remembers even though you may not want to remember them." And with that, Sam looked over at his friend, smiling confidently. "See, now you know why I'm going to Tech next year to do pre-med. I dig this shrink shit."

"That's good, Dr. Smug, only a couple of problems with your analysis," Josh said as Sam began looking for parking places in the neighborhood around TJ. "First of all, I'm flashing back to events I was never at."

"But that's your subconscious…see, it remembers what you don't."

"Well, it's got a hell of a memory—not to mention it must be a lot older than me also, considering these flashbacks are from a hundred years ago." Josh then opened the door and jumped out just as Sam cut off the engine. "Play that one in your head for a bit and get back to me on it," Josh gloated, having for once astonished his friend.

"We need to talk about this, Josh. This could be serious," Sam said, reaching over to lock Josh's door and his.

"You're right about that, Dr. Sam; in these flashbacks I've almost been shot a couple times and I don't know if it would hurt or kill me or what. Lucky thing, too, as good a shot as them Rebs were."

They both chuckled at that considering Sam wouldn't know the Battle of Malvern Hill from Malvern Ave. The former was about 25 miles west of the actual site and probably unrelated in spite of the name. Actually even with Josh's interest in the Civil War, neither of them had any forebears with any connection at all with the war. Both of their families came from Europe and did not arrive in this country until long after the civil war was over. That was another point which made Josh's flashbacks that much more odd. He couldn't even say there was a relative trying to reach him from the past.

Josh bid his friend farewell at the top of the front steps to the school. Passing through the big oak doors, they headed off to separate homerooms—Sam to his no doubt quiet normal routine and Josh hesitantly and somewhat fearfully to Mrs. Sutton's room. Oh, how he longed for a little obscurity.

He decided to aim for nonchalance and just threw the door open and walked in, ignoring any would-be sarcasm or jokesters. Actually there were none. No one wanted to rile up Mrs. Sutton again, he figured. He walked to his seat and sat down, noticing that Penny was not in hers and in fact was nowhere in sight. *That's unusual,* he thought. She almost always was here before him, though riding with Sam had forced him to arrive a little earlier.

Just then she came in, carrying her books against her chest. A small pocket book hung from her wrist and her arms were folded in front of her as usual. Some girls did that to hide large breasts that they were not yet comfortable with. Penny was more athletic and did not have that problem. Josh watched her; she almost glided when she walked. Her eyes darted around the room and her smile flashed when she connected with a friend or acquaintance. Donald Jones was already in his seat but Josh was surprised to see that he didn't even look at Penny. In fact, if Josh didn't think his mind was playing tricks on him, he would have sworn Donald actually ignored her on purpose.

She walked right by the SOB and nodded towards him with an odd expression on her face—a sort of smile but not a warm one, like one that a person would offer while saying unflattering things between one's teeth like "hi, asshole!" Or at least that's what Josh would say; he figured Penny probably wouldn't be quite as crude. Of course he was probably inventing this all in his mind.

Penny sat down in her seat next to him and said, "Hi, Josh." She paused for a few seconds while she put something in her purse and then said with a slight twinkle in her eye, "Anything in store for us today I should know about? You know, with a little notice I could bring a camera and we could get some of this on film for the yearbook. Most school yearbooks are always starving for a little sensationalism."

She's pretty chipper this morning, he thought as he threw a quick glance in Donald's direction. He was sitting with his body turned in such a way that he could see neither of them.

"I'm not screwing anything up today. I just want to get through this week without another, uh, incident and look forward to the weekend."

Penny started to say something but Mrs. Sutton interrupted with announcements about school activities and such. As she spoke, she looked at Josh twice and smiled the second time. He was convinced that Mrs. Sutton actually liked him, but she wasn't the type to take any drama from a student that would make her less of a respected faculty member, especially in the eyes of her students. And that was okay. Josh liked that about her.

Sam's party was this weekend and some guys with girlfriends would bring them, others would bring a date and then some like Josh would come alone rather than just bring a girl for the hell of it. Sam currently didn't have a girlfriend and was not bringing a date. Josh had pictured it as his first date with Penny, but that seemed out of the question at this point.

"So you and Old MacDonald are going to do an archeological dig at the Chimberazzo Hospital this weekend," he said dryly with a hint of sarcasm.

"Well, not that it's any of your business, but no, I'm not digging anything with him this weekend or any other time." She glanced in Donald's direction for a split second when she said it.

"A lover's spat?" Josh kidded a bit, suddenly feeling very buoyant.

"Hardly," she said. "Not even if he was the only guy in the world."

Josh could barely keep his butt in the seat for wanting to jump up with a big *yes!* but he fought back the urge. He didn't know what had happened, but it didn't matter. Plus, he could see he'd irritated her with his little comment about "the Chimberazzo dig" so he chose silence as the better alternative.

"I don't suppose you are still looking for a partner to do the project with, are you?" she asked somewhat hesitantly.

Shit, I should keep my mouth shut more often, he thought.

"Actually I am," he said. "My friend Sam mentioned it this morning…"

"Well, that's okay you don't need to…"

"I had just finished telling him that I had hoped you and I were going to do it together, but that you had, uh, picked someone else."

Feeling a little guilty, she said, "Well, I don't want to butt in on a friendship. It's just a project."

"Right," he said slowly with a slight pause. "But I would very much like it if you would work on it with me." His honesty and a little vulnerability showed more than he had planned.

"Well, okay then. We only have two weekends to do this, so is there any chance we could work on it tomorrow?" she asked matter-of-factly.

"For sure," he said. "What time would you like to start and where?"

"You said we… uh, you, were going to, um, do it on Malvern Hill so I assumed we'd go there, wherever that is," she said, her face a little flushed.

The bell for first period rang.

"I'll pick you up at 10:00, if that's okay."

She paused as if lost in thought. "If you want to give me directions I can meet you there, Josh; it's not like this is a date or anything," she said with that little tiny stinger that can pierce armor.

"Well, I haven't been there in a long time so I'm not sure exactly how to tell you. It would be easier if you just ride with me." Josh fought to keep the disappointment of what she had just said from his voice. He knew this wasn't really a date either but he kept hoping to see some sort of spark in her eye or hear something in her voice that said maybe this was a little bit of a something. He hated that he blushed so easily.

Satisfied that she'd sent the right message, if somewhat sorry that she had obviously embarrassed him, Penny gathered her books and got up as everyone was doing the same.

Sitting in her next class, she thought about what had just happened. She had, in fact, been the one who asked Josh to join her and be her partner and in the end she had made it seem as though he had begged her to go out on a date. That was okay, though. She told herself that she was truly only asking him because she knew nothing of the Civil War and he appeared to know quite a lot.

Her antics about meeting him there were truthful but she was glad he insisted on picking her up because she had no idea if she could even get the car tomorrow. Penny's family only had one and on Saturdays there was no telling whether her parents might be running errands, going out, etc. Then again, if all that were true—Civil War expertise, needing a ride, not a date or anything—then why why did she have that feeling in her stomach again, those butterflies and a feeling of anticipation? She frowned a bit and opened her book as the teacher started reviewing the prior night's assignment.

Josh was sitting in trigonometry and wondering what he was feeling and maybe more importantly, trying to control it. *Okay, she's going with me tomorrow. That's good! Yet she squashed any plans I had of this being an official "beginning." That's bad! Okay, so it's not a date, but we'll be together and I'll have a chance to talk with her, impress her, and be in a position for my next move. That's good! All right, I'm sitting here not listening to Ms. Horton and she has just called on me and everyone is staring. That's bad!*

The bell that ended the last class sounded and Josh wound his way back to Mrs. Sutton's homeroom to put his books away. No homework for a change. He decided to not press his luck today so he put away his books in his desk, nodded at Penny who was doing the same, and said, " See you at ten, Pen." *Pen? Where did that come from?* Her puzzled expression undoubtedly asked the same question. That's what he was going to call her when they became a couple.

Visions of that moment, when he would first kiss her, played in his head as he walked towards Sam's car. The hot sun broke his concentration. It was a patented Richmond September afternoon. Remnants of summer were still all around. The smell of freshly cut grass and the faint sound of lawnmowers buzzing emanated from everywhere and yet nowhere in particular. The breeze that stirred on occasion felt welcomed by one's skin. The humidity made everything a little damp, especially Josh's back, which got sticky from sitting in those goofy desks. He noticed the big billowing clouds that seem to know just how to stay out of the sun's way and yet were building dark gray in the middle of their white edges. Another month and this would begin to look and feel a lot more like fall. He reached the Buick and Sam was already inside with the motor humming. Flinging himself into the front seat, he said, "Sorry, guy, but you'll have to get another expert to be your partner on Ivers' project. Penny's doing it with me."

"Well, can you be my partner and still do it with Penny?" Sam asked good-naturedly as he pulled away from the curb into the rush of other students, mostly seniors, driving their own or their parents' cars.

"Very funny."

"Yeah, I bet you wish, huh?"

"Hey, it's not like that. I really like her."

"Okay, that's good, but you can do it with people you like, too, you know! I read that somewhere....even people who like each other can—"

"Spare me. Shit. First of all don't forget that it's just a project, not a relationship," Josh said, still feeling the disappointment in his chest.

"Hmm, that sounds a lot like something a girl would say," Sam observed as he adjusted the rear view mirror to keep Karen Mossberger in his view as they crept past her in the traffic.. "Hmm, she is really something, isn't she?" he mumbled, not taking his eyes off the mirror.

Josh looked back over his shoulder and spotted her. He knew Sam was interested in her but she had a boyfriend, at least for the moment, so Sam was also a wishful thinker at this point.

"You're right on both counts. Karen is cute and Penny did say that—about the project versus relationship thing. I can't seem to get her to acknowledge that there could be something more to this than just schoolwork."

"Well, as you know, I have all sorts of advice to give on these things…"

"Yes, I know you do; that's why you're having to look at Karen in your rearview mirror and are about to nail Mr. Poletts in two seconds."

Sam slammed on the brakes, even though he was only going a couple miles an hour, and Poletts was a good fifteen feet in front of him, crossing the street between traffic. The car screeched and jerked violently; naturally, this drew lots of laughs from kids on both sides of the street, including Karen, who recognized the car and Sam. "Goddamit, Josh, now you've made me look like an idiot to everybody out here, especially Karen."

"Well, at least Mr. Poletts is relieved," Josh said smiling as he nodded at the teacher, who was taking down Sam's license plate number and was about to pick up the briefcase he had just dropped. All his papers and books had spilled when it flew open after hitting the street.

He glared at the boys throughout the ordeal. Josh always felt a sense of satisfaction when he could put Sam in his place, just a little. He loved Sam like a brother, but his friend sometimes made him feel a little less than smart. "So what are you doing this weekend, besides having the party tomorrow night? Any idea how many people are coming?"

"Not much, really; my parents are looking at apartments and I committed to cleaning the house for the party. Shit, I told my mom cleaning afterwards makes a lot more sense. She said, 'Sam honey, you're gonna do that, too!' You know my parents want to fly the nest when I go to school. I think they're looking forward to that as much as I'm looking forward to going away to school. Looks like I'm going to go to Tech. Tuition is reasonable and it's getting a really good name," Sam said as he one-armed a right turn, lacing his fingers on the wheel and letting it slide back around.

"You still thinking about Syracuse?"

"Yeah, as long as I think I'm interested in communications. The Maxwell School of Communications is one of the best, so I'm still leaning that way, or Tech if I decide to stay closer to home. I think my grades will get me to either one if I can do shit on my boards. Then again, sometimes I wonder if that's really what I want to do. They say many of us will change majors at least once, if not more, but Syracuse is expensive so I know my dad will want me to stick it out if I'm going there for Maxwell. We'll see."

That night after dinner, Josh sat in his room, listening to the radio and thinking about what a goofy week it had been, when suddenly his dad came in with the rifle and sat on the bed.

"You know, Josh, looking at this thing makes you wonder where it's been and what it's seen, doesn't it?" He eyed the rifle with a sort of reverence. "Do you think I should just hang it over the fireplace in the den, stand it in the foyer, or what?"

"Well, dad," Josh said, not looking directly at the steel and wood piece, " I wouldn't be at all surprised if that rifle has caused—I mean, *seen*—some pretty tough times. You might want to protect it by putting it in the closet and just showing it on special occasions." The last thing he wanted was to have to walk by it or sit in front of it everyday. Talk about tempting fate.

"In the closet? No way. For what I paid for this, I'm going to display it out in the open, unless maybe you want it in your room."

Josh dropped the record he was getting ready to throw on his hi fi. Its cardboard cover bounced off the record changer and hit the floor rolling. Chasing the black disc across the room, he said, "Uh, you know, dad, on second thought, standing in the foyer might be a good place for it."

Six hours later, Josh awoke suddenly, thinking that he smelled rain. He did smell rain and he felt damp all over. *What the hell?* He reached for the light on his table but there was none. In fact, he realized he wasn't lying in his bed. *Oh Christ,* he thought. He was afraid to even sit up. He just laid there, listening. He could hear faint sounds like leaves rustling and a sort of crackling. Then he noticed a very pungent smell, almost like when he was at Boy Scouts camp, where no one showered very often. He reached out and felt something. It was material: canvas! He was in a tent, of all things. *Oh shit. Not again.* He sat upright and the first thing he noticed was a body lying next to him. *Who the hell was that?* He didn't dare disturb him because the only thing worse than not knowing who it was would be knowing who it was!

He could see that there was a flap on the tent and he opened it slightly. The crackling sound was coming from a campfire only yards from where they were lodged. He could see many other fires in either direction and some a long ways across the field that stretched out in front of them. Most of the fires appeared to be dying out gradually. He could also see stacks of rifles in little pyramids all up and down the campsite, including his dad's in front of his tent; but there were no soldiers that he could see in any of the firelight. They were all undoubtedly snoring away in their white canvas tents, of which he could see hundreds, maybe thousands. Speaking of snoring, the sound of the heavy breathing of whoever that was next to him began to grate on his nerves—not to mention it was obvious that the fellow had not flossed and brushed or showered before turning in.

Suddenly, a thunderous fart split the air. "God damn, man, I thought your *breath* was bad," Josh whispered between his teeth; and with that he dug in his heels and pushed himself backwards from under a rubber-like blanket that covered him to the back of the tent so his head stuck out from under the canvas. *Jesus, what the hell are they feeding these guys? Maybe they should infiltrate it into the Rebs' rations at night. A few rounds of these and the Rebs would probaly surrender on the spot! I'd save my bullets for the cooks if it was me!*

Once Josh was able to breathe fresh air, his head cleared a bit and he focused on the obvious. He was back here again. He had hoped it was over, that he was done with this shit. Was this Malvern Hill? Was this before or after the battle? Before or after Sergeant Pelter's death? Was he flashing back sequentially or randomly? Shit, he had no time for this; he was seeing Penny tomorrow, today—whenever—to study this very war! With that he felt a raindrop hit him on the cheek, then another and another. He could hear the rain growing in intensity, hitting the leaves, clopping on the canvas and hissing as it hit the nearby campfire.

Thunder rumbled in the distance and lightning lit up the tree leaves a sort of gray green. *Shit!* He slid back under the canvas into the tent. There didn't appear to have been any more human howitzer blasts in there since he'd scrambled out on his back. Not exactly possessing the ambiance of a Holiday Inn, but the space was at least bearable again. Josh began thinking in earnest about this situation and panic began to build. Lying in a tent with a "tent buddy" of unknown origin in a strange place in a strange time—this was not his idea of adventure, though he could think of a few idiots in school who would probably trade places with him gladly.

The inside of the tent lit up with a blast of lightning; the thunder accompanying it was deafening. Josh squeezed his eyes tight and ducked his head under the blanket. *Hell, no one could sleep through that,* he worried, assuming he must now have an awake "bunkmate" who would be equally curious about him… or did he know him already? Listening to the rumbling thunder, Josh peeked above the blanket to see who this character was, but saw instead the familiar light from the streetlight shining through his bedroom window, which was streaked with rain. Lightning flashed again but it didn't bother Josh. He took a deep breath and mumbled something about a promise to God that he would do anything for him… anything.

CHAPTER VII
Malvern Hill

It was Saturday morning and Penny stirred slightly, realizing with great satisfaction that there was no school today; she started to doze off again. Then she remembered what day it was and opened one of those almond-shaped eyes towards the clock on her nightstand. 8:00 a.m. She stretched and then relaxed, lying there thinking about the day. There was no need to rush. She wasn't going to be putting makeup on—well, maybe a little. Her hair would be pulled back and just a simple pair of jeans and a top would do. *Remember, this is not a date,* she repeated to herself.

What exactly was this? She hadn't made up her mind yet. She had to do this project and with a partner, so from that perspective it was just routine. Her friend Sharon had told her that she was nuts for pairing up with Josh, even if just for a project.

"And I suppose you would have told him to get lost had he asked you," Penny said.

"Well, first of all, he would never ask me," she said somewhat jealously, in spite of herself. "He doesn't even know my name. It's you he's after; we all know that. And besides, he's Jewish; I don't need that hassle with my parents. They get after me enough as it is for some of the 'birdbrains" as my dad calls them, that come to pick me up; but at least we all believe in the same God! Your parents would not be happy if they thought for a minute that you might intend to date Josh."

"I never said a word about planning on going out with him. Second, I decided a long time ago that when the right guy comes along at the right time, whoever and whatever he is, that is how it will be. I'm not marrying anyone someday for my parents' sake. I'm the one who will live with him, make love with him, bear our children with him, and hopefully grow old with him, so it's my choice." Still, she knew it wouldn't be easy if it ever came to that. She would have to think long and hard before letting that happen. She remembered Sharon's silent expression, sort of a mixture between envy and fear.

Enough thinking; time to get up. She threw back the covers and climbed out of bed, noticing it was now close to 8:30. Her pale blue oxford cloth shirt (actually, her older brother's) hung down to her mid-thighs. As she zipped into the bathroom, she looked at her legs appreciatively. She had a nice body and though she wasn't tall, her legs appeared longer than they really were. She was not dark skinned but not fair either. Her tan from the summer was fading but still noticeable. She could still see the remants of her tan lines as she quickly dropped her clothes in the bathroom and stepped into the shower.

Thirty minutes later, Penny appeared in the kitchen dressed in faded jeans, a pink cotton top that made her skin look that much more tan, and a pair of white sneakers with white socks. The smell of bacon and eggs floated to her nostrils.

"Hmm, smells good in here," she said to her mom, who was standing at the sink washing a few dishes and putting them in the rack.

"Morning, Hon," she said without turning around. "Hungry? I can make you some breakfast—eggs? There's bacon I just made a little while ago."

"No, thanks; I'll just pop some toast in the toaster and pour myself some coffee and juice."

A few minutes later, Penny was sitting at the table munching away.

"Hey, mom—what would you do if I ever came home with a boyfriend who wasn't Catholic?" She thought this would be a good way to ease into the conversation.

Her mother turned around to face her. "Penny, why would you even ask such a question? Is there something your dad and I should know?" She arched an eyebrow as she sat down across from Penny.

"Not at all! Just wondering. You know we talk about these kinds of things between classes and after school at the Clover Room." *Hmmm… the idea of peppermint chocolate flake in a sugar cone just might derail the conversation,* she thought.

"To be honest, it's not something I've given much thought to," her mom fibbed, "but your dad and I , though we aren't all that religious, certainly want you to one day settle down with a nice Catholic boy and have a family. There are worse things, though, than marrying a Lutheran or other kind of Protestant, I suppose."

"And what about a Jewish boy?" asked Penny as she pushed the butter around on her plate with her knife, not looking directly at her mother.

"Penny! Why are you asking these questions—and especially *that* one!" her mom exclaimed while facing her daughter squarely and looking directly into her beautiful eyes. " I have the utmost respect for the Jewish religion and those who practice it. They have survived a history that shames most of the civilized world. But culturally they are different and marriage these days is hard enough without those complications."

"Oh, mom, no real reason at all. We have a history project to do for school on the Civil War and we're supposed to do it with a partner, so I'm doing it with Josh Gershwin and he's Jewish."

"Josh Gershwin? Why not with one of your girlfriends?" her mom wondered, her voice rising a bit.

"Mr. Ivers thought it would be best if we paired off so that those of us who don't really know much about the war would have a chance to work with someone who does. I don't know a thing about the war and Josh is from Richmond and seems to have some interest in it and he asked me." Technically that was true. He had asked her or implied he was going to before the Donald fiasco. The fact she had asked him was really just a return to that same conversation.

"Why did he ask you, Penny? Is he thinking it could lead to something else?"

Ouch, Penny didn't want to get into this kind of discussion. Mainly because she had no answers and didn't want to speculate. She didn't want to have to defend herself when there was no need to. "Oh mom, don't worry. He probably knew we were relatively new in Richmond and thought it was a nice gesture. Besides, you know my plans. College next fall. No undue complications, especially with guys—Protestant, Jewish, or otherwise at this stage in my life."

"Uh huh. Well, the churches and synagogues are clogged with weddings of kids who said they weren't interested in getting married anytime soon…marriages for all kinds of reasons…." She let the last statement just hang there for emphasis.

Penny ignored her mom's obvious between-the-lines commentary on the danger of premarital sex.

"Oh, look at the time! Josh is picking me up in a few minutes," she said as she screwed the top back on the orange juice.

"Picking you up? Why don't you just meet him there...*there*? Where is *there*?"

"We're going to Malvern Hill battlefield and I have no idea where it's at other than on the southeast side of Richmond. I also didn't know if you would let me have the car today either."

Satisfied with the explanation, her mom said, " Ok, hon. Sorry about the short lecture. I think you really do want to stay focused on getting into a good school next year and I know you can't sit at home all the time working on schoolwork. I guess I shouldn't complain. Here you are going out with a boy, and it's to do class work. You know your great great grandfather Charles was in the Civil War fighting for the Confederacy under Stonewall Jackson, I believe. He wrote letters home to the family about his experiences including once being captured for a time and his escape. I wish I knew what became of them. I just remember that the story goes that he always felt in debt to a Union soldier who saved his life and he always said he would repay him no matter how long it took. To tell you the truth, I'm not sure he ever did though, I think he lost track of him after the war. "

Penny fidgeted as she listened to her Mom, waiting for Josh to pick her up. Mrs. Collingsly detected her daughter's impatience and let it go at that.

"Oh well, I'm sure Josh will provide you with plenty of insight and information for your project Penny. Just be sure to keep the focus on the project," she said with raised eyebrow.

"Thanks, Mom," Penny said with a sigh as she saw Josh pulling up. As she suspected, he didn't just blast the horn but started to get out. Thinking that she'd rather not get into introductions and all that, she bounded for the door, saying, "See you later, Mom" and out she went, meeting him halfway down the walk.

"Hi, Pen," he said. *There it was again: nobody called her "Pen"! It didn't bother her, but then again it did. Too familiar? Did she like it but didn't want to admit it? Damn, she thought, I'm losing my mind worrying over stuff like this.*

"Hi, Josh," she said, running over to the car and opening her door before he could do it for her. It was a long, black Oldsmobile whose seats were a very plush, light gray; the car was almost limousine looking. "Nice car," she said, admiring the inside.

"Well, my dad always thinks it's better to buy a used car 'cuz he says you get more for your money. Guess that's true if you can keep 'em running. This car was an executive's company car. It's a couple years old and we've only had it for a few months. Rides nice and has all the power stuff and air conditioning," he said, pushing the chrome button on the dash.

The sound of air blowing through the vents came up and the cool dry air took the Richmond September humidity out of the car. It was around ten o'clock but it was already humid and seventy degrees. It was going to be a warm fall day.

"So, we're off to Malvern Hill?" she asked while looking at him and picking up her spiral notebook from her lap; she opened it to a blank page that had a pen hanging on it. "I have no idea what that really is other than you said there was a battle fought there? A big one or a little, uh, skirmish?" She settled back in the plush gray leather cushion.

"Well, I'm no expert, but I did a little reading in one of my dad's books. Want to know a little about the background?" he asked, as he looked over at her and wondered if he should pinch himself. *She is a great-looking girl, no doubt about it. She looks good in pink*—he blushed as he thought what she might really look like in the pink!

The scent of her perfume floated around him and made him a little lightheaded. She always seemed so relaxed and confident. If it was an act, it was a great one. He felt nervous and was sure it showed.

"Sure, she said but do you know how to get there?"

"Yes, we're going out on Laburnam Road, south to highway 5 and then east to the battlefield. It's about a half-hour drive."

"Okay," he said. "Real quick: here's what happened out there. Robert E. Lee, Commander of the Army of Northern Virginia of the Confederate States, believed he could destroy the Union army under George McClellan at Malvern Hill and free Richmond from the threat of McClellan's forces. That would end the threat to the South's capital, and, of course, end the war. There had been a series of battles fought during that week which today are called 'The Seven Days' Battles.' Nobody had won any great victory but Lee had succeeded in stalemating McClellan. McClellan grew impatient and concerned for his ability to supply his men, which were a hundred miles from Washington. As usual, he imagined himself outnumbered, which he wasn't, and began to withdraw his forces on the way to Harrison's Landing, where his supply train was nearby. On the way, he occupied a hill called—you guessed it—Malvern Hill.

"The Union canons ringed the hill, making a direct attack by Confederate infantry a very dangerous move. As you will see, it's an open field with a long gradual slope to the ridge. Most of it, though, is in the open with no cover for half a mile. Lee needed to take out the artillery guarding the ridge and tried, but as his canons were rolled out to get a sighting, they were knocked out by the Union guns. Confederate communication wasn't the best, and eventually one brigade moved forward on its own and the other brigades misread this as the signal for the beginning of the attack and so they attacked also. I guess in the end it was pretty much a slaughter. In fact, one of the confederate generals said that it wasn't a war, but murder. The Union artillery was especially effective against troops in the open.

The Confederates were pushed back with heavy losses. McClellan continued the retreat to Harrison's Landing instead of following up on the victory, which was typical of the way he commanded. In the end, McClellan, who actually had superior numbers, could most likely have outlasted Lee and moved on Richmond and taken our little city then and there and maybe ended the war in 1862. But caution got the best of him and he withdrew and lost the opportunity. Instead, the war lasted another three years. So while Malvern Hill was a bad defeat for the Confederates overall, the Seven Days' Battle was a victory because McClellan didn't take Richmond."

He looked over at Penny, thinking she would be dozing off by now, but she was actually wide awake and taking notes. He was impressed.

"You seem to know a lot about this," she said, trying to hide her amazement at how easily he had recounted all of that and how understandable he had made it.

He didn't respond for a moment as he felt a chill and thought he heard thunder. But as he looked up, he didn't see a cloud in the sky.

"Did you hear that?" he asked apprehensively.

"Hear what?" Penny looked out of her window and cocked her head as she strained to listen.

"Uh, well, it was a rumbling sound like thunder, but obviously it couldn't have been that. Maybe it was a backfire. Anyhow, here it is up ahead," he said, changing the subject and pointing to a place on the side of the road. He pulled over into an area for tourists and they got out and walked to where there were gray metal historical markers and several large canons neatly lined up. Penny walked over and read the markers' account of what had happened here and what its significance had been. Longer and more detailed than Josh's description, but no more informative.

She walked over to Josh, who was standing behind the row of canons. The pair stood silent for a moment as they gazed out to where the canon muzzles faced. It was a long, open, rectangular field of green with thick woods on either side of it and down at the far end. She could see now how it would be tough to walk up even this mild grade with no cover and gunfire coming down the slope from where they stood. She shuddered to think of thousands of Confederates marching slowly from the surrounding woods right into the faces of these canons and the Union infantrymen. She wondered how men were found to volunteer for such things, knowing there was little medical help if they were wounded.

She turned to say something to Josh but he was looking off into the distance and he motioned for her to walk with him; they moved out in front of the guns. There really was very little here to signify what had happened. She wasn't even sure if they were permitted to walk across the area. But she could see he was determined and so she moved with him. He walked quickly with a focus, almost as if he knew where he was going. He slanted off to the right side of the field towards the woods. They walked a short distance as his angle took them off to the side of the field where the woods met the open field. Stopping some thirty or forty yards from the area of the artillery placement, Josh sat down on the grass and rubbed his eyes and his temples as though he had a headache.

"Are you all right, Josh?" Penny asked. She began to wonder what he was up to.

Just then Josh stood up and walked to a spot a few yards away and said calmly, "This is where Sergeant Pelter was killed. I was over there, lying face down after he had cursed at me and knocked me over to keep me from being shot. He was trying to rally the troops when he himself was cut down. I heard him shout, 'You don't disappoint Sergeant Pelter today,' and then he was hit in the chest and knocked over like a bowling pin." Josh was sweating and motioning as he spoke, pointing to the ground not far from Penny and then pointing to where he had just said he'd been lying in the grass.

"Oh right, Josh, and where do you keep your little time machine—in your garage? Or do you just will yourself back to any time and place you'd like? You know I'd really like to interview Joan of Arc at the stake; can you take me to her, Josh?" Penny was not sure if he was trying to make her look silly or was it that sense of humor again—but then she noticed the serious expression on his face. She had obviously hurt his feelings. Sighing, she said, "Josh, what on earth are you talking—"

"I ran to those woods over there and took cover with a bunch of other Union soldiers until the tide of the battle changed and the Rebels were pushed back," he said, pointing and moving towards the woods. I moved out slowly, clutching my dad's rifle after the Union soldiers rallied from the woods and I tried to give water to a guy wounded in the leg right over there. Out of nowhere, a wounded Rebel then came at me, swinging his empty rifle, and he managed to knock me down and out. Everything went black and then the flashback was over and I woke up in my bed at home!"

Penny shook her head. "Flashback? Josh, this is all pretty weird, like a… uh… I'm not sure what…" She paused as she stood up and walked around as if to clear her head, but she was mindful not to step on the spot where Sergeant Pelter or whomever was killed. *Jeez,* she shuddered, *he's even got me acting weird.*

"Don't you, remember, Penny, the other day in school when Mr. Ivers had Mr. Pelter talking to us over the intercom about the battles around Richmond and I jumped up and went a little nuts?"

Penny stopped walking, stood thinking, and said, "Yes, I remember, and *nuts* is definitely a good description." The name Pelter did sound familiar and she certainly remembered the man who addressed them—and who could forget Josh's antics.

"Penny, I know you think I'm nuts, but believe me, this is as confusing to me as it is to you."

I doubt that, she thought. Josh sat her down and started talking about his flashbacks and filled her in on all the details of what had been happening to him. He even recounted the night in the rainy tent with the blast from the sleeping "bunkmate" that drove Josh to stick his head out from under the tent for fresh air. She couldn't help but laugh at that with a blush. When Josh had finished, Penny sat stunned with an expression on her face that Josh couldn't read. She thought long and hard for something to say. She didn't want to insult him and yet she wasn't about to buy into any of this yet.

Finally, after a long uncomfortable silence, she said, "Well, Josh, I think maybe we've seen enough of Malvern Hill."

"You think I'm a loony bird, don't you, Penny?" Josh started to walk back to the car. Penny caught up with him and put her hand on his sleeve.

"Josh, I don't know what to make of this. You can't expect me to just buy into all of this matter-of-factly. Let's see… Well, maybe, why not! I mean, it's just a routine day for anyone, right? Touching a gun and waking up in a Civil War battle, flashing back to the inside of a tent with a bunkmate who— ugh, never mind. Although I have to hand it to you: that is pretty bizarre even for you to make up."

At that point, Josh walked quickly towards the car. Penny was instantly sorry for the cynicism in her voice. She ran up behind him and pulled his arm back towards her. As she did, he turned towards her, avoiding her eyes, and she suddenly had a rush of feelings that made her reach out and pull him towards her. They stared at one another for several long seconds and suddenly she leaned forward and gently kissed him. He was so surprised that he almost fell against her. The soft warmth of her lips and the smell of her perfume made him dizzy. Penny pulled back, trying to regain her composure. Seeing his face flushed and feeling her own cheeks burning, she thought, *Damn! Why did I do that?!* Still feeling the trace of his lips on hers, she didn't want to think about the answer.

They drove in silence for some time. It just sort of hung there in the car. Josh couldn't help but think how great everything was.. He went from being convinced that she thought he was an idiot to wondering if she felt sorry for him, but now he wondered if there was more to Penny's emotions than that. Penny thought that if there was an idiot in this scenario, then it was her. She opened up her armor and exposed her vulnerability. She had gone against her own principles of keeping her distance from this boy—this boy whom she was convinced had some kind of chemistry that affected her at a time when she was determined to not let romance happen.

"Penny," Josh finally broke the silence, "I'm not exactly sure what happened back there. I probably should never have told you about all of that and made myself look like a ranting idiot. But when you took my arm and kissed—"

"Josh, that was just a reaction to seeing that I had hurt you. Don't put any significance to that." Josh felt a burning inside.

"I don't have time in my life for that stuff right now," she added. I've got a mission to accomplish during this year and that is to keep my grades high enough to get into UVA with scholarship help. That's it; that's my focus. We're just friends—new friends, actually—and we need to finish this project; and maybe, if I don't get trampled by a horse in one of your, uh, flashbacks, we will still be friends."

That relieved the tension momentarily. They drove on in silence. As Josh drove up in front of her house wanting to talk more, Penny quickly jumped out of the car and announced, "I have a book from the library on Malvern Hill. I'll write up my notes and give them to you and you can hopefully add yours. Then we'll review it one time to put it together to hand it in at school. Okay, Josh?"

She was halfway to her door by then, not waiting for an answer. Josh just shrugged, feeling disappointed that she had said there was nothing to their first small moment of intimacy.

She closed the door behind her and quickly turned to see the sadness in his face as he pulled away from the curb. She let out with a confused sigh, tossed her notebook on the chair, and darted to her room.

CHAPTER VIII
Surprises

She lay on the bed, thinking about what had just happened. *Was he loony? Who knows. Was she falling for him? How could she be? Not after one kiss and all those antics lately.*

But her body was not rational. It was reacting to the touch of his lips on hers and the feel of his arms and was making her tingle from head to toe. *Enough of this,* she thought, and bounded out off the bed and into the living room to get the Malvern Hill book. She planned to finish writing up her notes and then call Josh to discuss the project only—and they would finish it.

She couldn't focus after half an hour of trying, so she decided to walk to the library and work on her assignment there. She decided to pull a few more books and do some more research and suddenly she came across something that brought a chill over her. It was one of those eyewitness accounts excerpted from a Union soldier's letter written to his family, telling that he had been in a battle but that he was fine. "…and we was all divin' for cover as the Rebs was a-sweepin' the field. 'Bout then we got some reinforcements and the battle fortunes began to swing our way. Pelter jumped to his feet and shouted for us to do the same, yelling for us to not disappoint him today' and that's when a Reb mini-ball hit him in the chest. Knocked him flat over backwards like a damn bird shot off a fence rail." Penny's eyes were riveted to the page but her mind was rushing back to replay Josh's words at Malvern Hill. He had said that Pelter cursed at him and knocked him down—that Pelter jumped up and tried to rally the troops and got hit in the chest. A wave of chills washed over her, giving her goose bumps. Josh had said that the sergeant had told them not to disappoint him that day, just before he got knocked over like a bowling pin—or a bird on a rail!

This is just too weird. Is this just a bizarre coincidence? Or is Josh up to a prank, having read this same book? To make himself seem weird? Why? But any other explanation was impossible!

Josh sat in the car in front of his house, enjoying the cooling breeze from the air conditioning. He sought to plan his next move. He probably should have been more concerned about the flashbacks and how and what to do about them, if anything. Instead, he wallowed in self-pity because it was Saturday and he was going to Sam's party alone.

He felt really alone at that moment. He gazed over at the passenger side of the car and wished Penny was still there. He caught sight of Brushes watching him from under a bush in the front yard. The hound rose, stretched, and slowly ambled his long, thick body and stubby legs towards the car and sat down between the house and the car, his tail wagging slightly. After another few minutes he began barking at Josh, sort of a *well, are you coming or going, guy?!*

That was enough for Josh; he didn't need his dog giving him grief today too. He shifted into gear and slowly drove off, though he had no idea where he was going. A quick look in the rearview mirror revealed Brushes ambling back to his spot under the bush.

Sorry, boy, Josh thought guiltily. He drove around for a while, passing Dot's bakery on Cary Street, where he smelled fresh cake or something and before he knew it, he was very close to Penny's house. And just as he had made up his mind that this was silly and that he needed to go home, he spotted Penny a half a block away walking back from the library. Panic gripped him as he suddenly realized that he didn't want her to see him, driving around like some moony-eyed kid. He was a block from her house and quickly pulled over amongst a few parked cars. *Too late.* He could see that she noticed him. She quickened her pace and headed right for him.

Penny crossed the street and walked up to the car, carrying some books and notebooks. Josh leaned across the passenger seat and opened the door for her and she slid onto the seat, closing the door gently. She sort of shifted in the seat for a second, facing forward, then turned her head toward him with an amused if puzzled look.

"Hi," she said, smiling slightly and looking directly into his eyes. "So you forgot where your house is, huh?" She smiled faintly. "Had to come find me so I could give you directions, eh? Guess you forgot I've never been there, so I'm no help at all," she teased.

She isn't angry with me? Josh wondered. She was actually smiling slightly.

"Uh, well. . ."

She shifted her body to face him and said in a somewhat mocking tone, "Well, what then? I said we should finish our write-ups and compare notes. What did you do? Finish them in the car on the way over? Let me see them." She glanced over her shoulder as if she expected to find them in the back seat, but obviously not.

"I, well, I haven't started them yet. Is that what you were doing?" He glanced down at the books in her lap.

"Yes. After this loon I was with dropped me off, I went to the library to write up my notes."

She was looking directly into his eyes and he was having difficulty concentrating as those flashing eyes just mesmerized him. She was still smiling though—very important if she was going to be calling him names, he thought, as he squirmed at the word *loon.*

"And you know what?" she asked without pausing. "I was so confused with my own notes, and all that, uh, stuff you threw at me out there"—now she sounded angry; Josh shrank backwards a bit—"that I started looking for more information on our little Malvern Hill. And do you know what I found in a book on that subject, Mr. Gershwin?"

Uh oh, this does not sound good, Josh thought, as he shrank back even further.

"By chance, I found a book with an eyewitness account of the death of our Sergeant Pelter. It was in a letter written by a Union soldier to his family in Wisconsin letting them know that he had survived the battle." She stopped dead there and just looked at him—right into his dazed eyes, trying to ignore his good looks and the heart she was beginning to feel beat faster.

"Private David Striker—sound familiar? Did you know him?" she barked, half in jest and half in earnest.

Haltingly, Josh answered, " No, I didn't. What did the le... letter say?" He was curious now.

"Oh, you mean you never read it?" She was testing him.

"Read it? What is that supposed to mean?" Then it hit him. "Oh, I see: You think I made all that up based on some account I read in a book, huh?" Anger began to course through him. "You think I purposely made myself out to look like an idiot to you and everyone else in school? Why would I do something like that?"

She glanced around a little sheepishly and shrugged her shoulders and then looked back at him. "Well you got me there, Josh. I don't know."

"You think I did all that just to get your attention, don't you, Miss Collingsly." He realized he'd never used her last name before. Refocusing, he continued: "Hey, I might think you are really cute but don't think I would go and—"

"What did you say?" She cut him off suddenly, her eyes glancing down at his mouth.

Caught in mid-sentence, he lost his thought. Before he could answer, she decided she didn't need a repeat. She had heard it. She thought, *if he thinks she's cute, that's nice; but she didn't need to stroke her ego and put him on the spot.* She had already practically accused him of making up his story. Obviously, whatever the truth was, he was struggling with it inside.

"Never mind, Josh; I shouldn't have put you on the defensive like that. Sorry." He was more sensitive than any boy she had known—and more vulnerable, it seemed. That would attract her to him if she let it. She had a lot of emotions and mixed feelings in her head and body right now. She should pull the door handle and go—now!

He looked at her for a moment. Neither of them spoke. Their eyes locked.

He put his arm around her waist and pulled her towards him. Their faces were both a little flushed from the conversation. He leaned towards her and brushed her lips with his, soft at first and then harder. Her lips responded by opening slightly. He could taste her lipstick and smell her hair spray. They kissed for a long moment with his arms gathering her in. He pulled back slightly to look into her eyes, which were only half open, and then kissed her again, softly at first, not wanting to overwhelm or scare her.

"You know we have a very special chemistry, you and I. I knew it the first time I saw you," he said, kissing her softly again.

"Oh, is that right, Mr. Blue Belly? We southern girls don't take kindly to you boys in blue," she said with a sultry sort of half smile, her eyes fixed directly on his. And with that, their lips met again, harder. Each could feel the force of the other as their passion increased. Her body felt so solid in his arms. He had a feeling he had never experienced before, almost as though he was unaware of anything but her lips and her smell. For Penny, this was beyond anything she had ever experienced and she responded to his touch, feeling a sort of wild panic and yet comfort at the same time. He kissed the side of her neck and ran his fingers up to her hair at the back of her neck. He could feel her tremble, or was that him? Suddenly her panic won out and she pushed him back.

"Oh damn," she said. She gasped for breath and straightened herself. "I can't let this happen now; I told you that. I've got to go." A tear ran down her cheek as she grabbed her books and opened the door and ran from the car. He watched her as she covered the block or so to her house quickly and did not stop as she flung open the door and disappeared inside.

It was already three o'clock. They had sat there for a half hour and yet it seemed no longer than a minute. Josh was driving home but he didn't notice anything. The car must have been on auto pilot because the only thing he was thinking about was what just happened. This had sure been an up and down day. It started with hope, if not expectation. Then it went into a spin—with disaster written all over it.

Now, who knows. She definitely felt something for him. She was fighting it and might tell him to get lost tomorrow, but he had made a big impact on her. His mind went back over the past half hour, over and over again. No matter what happened, he was hooked.

Penny sat on her bed, staring at herself in the mirror over her desk. She was beside herself, almost literally, as she saw another tear run down her cheek. It was a tear of anger this time. She was mad at herself. She had these big plans and was going to go away to school—not to mention that he was Jewish and that would likely present big complications in itself.

And then she remembered the flashbacks and wondered what that was all about. Reincarnation? Was he truly a loon? But she could still smell his cologne and feel his body against her and his lips… *oh God, those lips!* She recalled the way that he had kept control of himself and taken it slowly. He was no loon. *Oh, shit!* She was going to have to resist all of this. *Just forget that it ever happened.*

Josh got home and found his parents getting ready to go out for dinner. "Want to go with us, Josh?" his mother asked. "We're going to Julian's for pizza."

"Uh, no, not hungry really. I have Sam's party tonight and I'll eat a bunch of stuff there." His mom looked at him as though he might be ill as he never turned down Julian's. This was the best pizza place in town; it was over by the train station on Broad Street.

"Will you be back by eight so I can have the car tonight?" he asked, looking at his dad hopefully.

"I'm sure we will. I mean, it's almost a full block to Sam's house; we wouldn't want you to get overtired," his dad sardonically observed.

"Well, it's not cool to walk to a party, no matter how close it is," Josh countered. "Plus, I can't walk that far with a case of High Life." Silence. "Just kidding, just kidding," he added before he got himself in trouble. "Actually, some of us may want to go for ice cream or pizza afterwards."

"Just be sure to call if you do so we'll know what you're up to," Mr. Gershwin said.

"Okay, you two, just hurry along now," Josh said in his best Jonathan Winters' "Granny" imitation, thinking, *Jeez, this sounds like an episode of Father Knows Best!!*

After they left him standing in the living room, he went to his room to figure out what he would wear that night as it was already five o'clock. He didn't see and definitely did not look for the rifle.

CHAPTER IX
The Next Chapter

It was a quarter past eight as he pulled up to Sam's house. It was a smallish white brick and frame house with a front yard he and Sam had played in and around since he could remember. As he entered the small living room, he was greeted by Sam's mom: a thin graying woman who, like his mom, had some difficulty accepting that their two boys were growing up.
"Hi, Josh; they're all out back," she said, gesturing over her shoulder with one hand and then quickly cupping her cigarette to catch an errant ash. Sam's mom was an even heavier smoker than Josh's mom.

He quickly walked through the den and out the sliding glass door to the back yard. He could hear the music before he even stepped through the doorway. There was a table next to a tool shed with a 45 rpm player on it turned up a bit loud for the little speaker to handle. The song "It Hurts To Be In Love" by Gene Pitney was playing and it reverberated in Josh's head as he waved and said hi to his friends and some people he didn't know that well. He had never gotten around to asking Penny, even though that was the one thing he wanted to do more than anything. Most of the kids came with no dates unless they were a going-steady item. He should have pushed Sam to invite her but he knew that Sam didn't really know Penny, as Josh himself had only met her recently.

Sam came up to him, shook his hand, and said, "Good to see you, Josh. Help yourself to a soda and something to eat." Josh reached into the cooler next to Sam and pulled out a tall grape soda, his favorite when unable to have a beer, and started to say what a great night for a party it was when he saw Sam's eyes dart over his shoulder towards the back door and then back to him. He instinctively looked back and saw Penny stepping tentatively through the door. His heart jumped and he quickly looked at Sam in surprise.

Sam saw her too. "Well, when your best friend has lost his mind, the least you can do is humor him a bit." Sam said as he raised his Pepsi and touched Josh's bottle.

"Well, I haven't filled you in on today's events but I will later," Josh said. "I may need to sort of give her a little space for a bit tonight," he added as he watched her out of the corner of his eye. He thought she spotted him and subtly meandered in a different direction. "I'm kind of surprised she came."

"You didn't tell her you captured Stonewall Jackson today, did you? I mean I haven't checked the six o'clock 1862 news lately, but I'm assuming us Rebs are still in the running," Sam joked. He waved to some other kids who had just arrived.

"Very funny. No, I took her to a battlefield today as part of that school project."

"Well, at least you didn't let a horse step on her," Sam said, unable to control a laugh.

"Okay, dufus,? go make the rounds." Josh then remembered amazingly that Penny had made a similar comment about continuing to be "just" friends if he didn't get her trampled by a horse.

Actually, it had been almost a full day since Josh had had an "attack" or whatever one would call it. Maybe he was done with all of that. He hadn't come near the rifle for that length of time either, and that might be a sign. He started to move in the direction of Penny, who was talking with a slightly overweight and over bearish Sarah. She was in Mrs. Sutton's class with them and had no doubt witnessed Josh's display on Thursday. As he approached them, Sarah nodded towards him while talking to Penny, and then smiled in his direction a bit too nicely.

Sarah's conversation level suddenly got a lot louder: "Oh, here comes our hero now. I hope you get one of those Union medals of honor, Josh!" All in earshot had a good laugh over that while Penny smiled uncomfortably, not quite ready yet to back him publicly but not wanting to see him embarrassed.

"Very funny, Sarah," Josh said. " Fact is you look just like one of the women camp followers I saw slipping from tent to tent on Army payday last week." With that, Sarah choked on her soda and dropped a Twinkie on Penny's foot that she was about to wolf down. A huge laugh went up from the crowd, most of them having heard about Josh's antics at school via friends if they hadn't been in the classroom themselves. She was clearly no match for Josh's wit. Penny quickly reached down to help Sarah retrieve the Twinkie but she had retreated to the shadows at this point. The string of party lights cast some big shadows all around as it was getting dark.

"Feeling pretty good about that one, are you, Sergeant Gershwin?" Penny asked with only a trace of a smile.

"Actually, I'm just a lowly Private; and no, I should have bit my tongue, but I couldn't resist. It's been a long up and down day."

"Well, maybe she had it coming," Penny said. "But she was in our class the other day when you, um…went bananas."

"Yeah, I know I'm the flashback fruitcake, aren't I?" Josh sighed, feeling a bit frustrated. The hi-fi began to play "Let It Be Me" by Jerry Butler and Betty somebody. Everyone started pairing up, dancing slowly on the grass, including Sam and Karen! Josh extended his hand to Penny. She stood looking at his hand for a few seconds. *It's just a dance,* she told herself, *nothing more.* She put her hand in his and he pulled her gently to him and they mixed in with the other couples.

They danced silently for a few minutes. Each could feel the warmth of the other's body. The smell of Josh's cologne fit perfectly with his natural ambiance and it pulled her to him. She felt like they were just sort of floating. He tried to think of something appropriate to say, but his mouth was dry and he was just overwhelmed for a time. With his arm around her waist and her forehead just under his chin, he leaned his head down a bit so his face was very close to hers.

"I did not know Sam invited you. You didn't mention it today," he said, just above a whisper.

"I wasn't sure I was coming, so I didn't want to bring it up."

"Actually, I'm surprised you did come. But thankful," he said, looking at her mouth and then her eyes.

"I need to meet some people and I needed a break from studying."

He figured that was her way of saying, *Don't read anything else into my being here.*

The song ended and they stood there not dancing and not moving either. Seconds later "The Twelfth of Never" by Johnny Mathis began playing and they just moved with the soft sound of his velvet voice.

Finally Josh had to say something or he thought he might burst. "Penny, today in the car....it was uh...I mean you are..." he paused. "I don't know what to say. I just think we could have something really good between us."

Mathis sang words that seemed so perfect if only Penny would ease up on herself, he thought.

Penny felt his breath on her cheek and his strong hand pressing the small of her back. *Of course, he had to be a good dancer too!* With no effort, he guided her to the music. In spite of everything she had said, she wanted to kiss him again.

A longing welled up inside of her. She was a virgin, as were all of her friends, but she was no wall flower. She had been to make-out parties and she had experienced necking and petting, but that was just having some fun, flirting and experimenting with her developing sexuality. But never during those times did she ever feel what she felt today and now.

He put his hand under her chin and lifted her face towards his and kissed her lips. She responded in kind and they danced for a moment, their lips and bodies pressed together, when suddenly panic welled up inside of her again just like before–that feeling as if she was losing control. She suddenly pulled back and looked at him.

"Josh, I can't do this. I can't. We have our religious differences and the family problems that would cause. You are sweet, but you have plans for school next year, as do I. Everything is going against us." She tried to keep calm so as not to draw attention to them, though couples dancing close couldn't help but hear.

She could see the disappointment in his eyes but she had summoned the courage to do this and she wasn't going to stop now. With that she pulled him over to the side where no one was dancing so as not to leave him standing out there and she kissed him on the cheek and walked briskly into the house.

Penny, in the midst of a huge silent struggle that raged within, walked through the house and out the front door, down the steps, and towards her car. She looked back once to see if Josh was coming after her but he was not. She had hurt him for sure. By the time she reached her car she was crying quietly, tears streaming down her face. As she drove home, she heard the sounds of "People" by Barbara Streisand floating up from the radio. When Babs crooned how special lovers are, Penny snapped the radio off and drove home in teary silence.

CHAPTER X
The Man

Josh awoke with a shiver. There was a chill in the air. As he lay half asleep, he thought, *Where did the warm weather go so quickly? Uh oh...where was he?* He sat up quickly. *Shit.* It was Friday night. It had been a week since Sam's party. A very long week. He had seen Penny every day in class and they had finished the Malvern Hill project but she was like a different person. No casual talk, no flashing, flirting eyes—no nothing. The extent of their conversations had been to wrap up the project and that was it. He tried his best to pull her back to him as he could not help but believe she felt much of what he felt but it didn't work. She was rarely alone, almost always with a girlfriend in the halls, cafeteria, everywhere. It was as if she had found the on/off button and had simply turned it off. As he turned all of this over in his mind, he began to focus his eyes and realized the reason he was cold was because he was sitting up in his underwear in a tent. A tent! He was staring up at a white-pointed roof made of grungy white canvas lying on a damp blanket with some facsimile of a sheet over him. Remembering his previous bout with a tent, he cautiously sniffed the air. Just a slightly musty smell greeted his nostrils this time.

Fortunately, he was alone in the tent. It was just after dawn but he could still see reasonably well inside. He looked around. At this point he pretty much accepted the fact that he was obviously having another flashback and that he could do nothing about it. For the moment at least, no one was blasting at him from an orifice or a gun and so he laid quietly, trying to digest where he might be and wondering if Penny was asleep right now. He noted that there was a uniform hanging from a strap or something on the other side of the tent. It looked brand new. Dark navy blue wool, he guessed.

Just then he heard quick footsteps and the flap of the tent snapped open with a pop and a sergeant stuck his head in the tent and said, "God Damn, boy, you better get yerself a- movin'. You think they is gonna wait on you farm boys today?"

"Farm boys? Today!!" Josh blurted out before thinking.

"By damn, boy, what'dya'do, go to sleep and forgit? Look, I don't know why the major named you part of this here honor guard for this here speech today, but he damned sure did and you damned sure ain't gonna be late and git my arse in trouble."

Josh's mind raced as he tried to assimilate what this might mean and if he was going to snap out of this at any moment. He blinked at the sergeant for a second and the skinny, tall man who looked to be in his mid-thirties or so with scraggly hair sticking out from under his Union cap started to come inside. That was all Josh needed. "Uh, yes sir," he said, as he sprang up (relieved to find he was wearing white long johns). "I'm on my way right this minute, sergeant. Now forgive me but one more time, where do I go…uh, where do I report?" Josh tried to sound casual as he lurched across the tent to get "his" uniform.

"You just stand your arse right in front of this tent and a wagon will pick you up 'long with the guards from the other companies too. You just do what yer told today and don't git me in no trouble, ye hear me, boy?"

"I do, sir. It's quite an honor to be part of this guard detail," Josh said, still trying to figure what this could be about, but not wanting to press his luck with the sergeant at this point.

"Yeah, well, maybe, but don't let it go to yer head 'cuz yer jest a wet behind the ears kid who is more luckier then anything to be breathing and not full of holes or missing an arm or leg. I thought this damn war would be over by now but I'm comin' up on the third damn Thanksgivin' away from my family in Wisconsin. Enough jabbing; get in uniform." With that, he turned his head and it vanished from the tent opening.

After a few frustrating minutes of trying to figure how to get the belt and sword on, Josh stepped from his tent handsomely dressed in a brand new dark blue uniform, still trying to figure out what event this might be at. Third Thanksgiving! *It has to be November of 1863,* he thought. The coat was heavy wool with brass buttons that buttoned up to the neck almost. He had a white collarless shirt under it, long navy blue pants that were a bit too short, and the most uncomfortable black boots. *Shit,* he thought, *somebody just sewed some pieces of leather together and then stuck a heel and flat sole on it.*

The sword and the scabbard were heavy and clumsy, swinging side to side. His powder box was also on the belt. It was full but he wouldn't have a clue what to do with its contents. He had his dad's trusty old rifle that was leaning against the tent as well. Between the sword and the rifle, he couldn't imagine walking anywhere very far. Not to mention the stupid pinching boots would bring him to his knees in no time flat. As he tried to figure out where he might be while smelling the clean crisp dawn air and seeing the twinkling remnants of campfires around him, he heard, then saw, a wagon coming toward him drawn by a single brown horse with four soldiers about his age in the open back. The driver (a civilian, it appeared, as he had no uniform) spoke something unintelligible to the horse, who stopped immediately.

"Ok, son, get in the wagon and take a seat."

"Yes, sir!" Josh said as he managed to find a place to stick his foot and to get some leverage to climb up into the wagon. The driver flipped the reins a bit and they were off. At first there was only the sound of the horse hooves on the soft, natural dirt road. Then, one by one, the other four boys began to talk about the war and how much they missed their families and homes. Josh just listened and nodded in agreement as they talked about their experiences. They were so young looking—skinny with dark hair or blonde hair, long and scraggly over their ears and coat collars. They barely needed to shave. As it turned out, some of them had fought at Gettysburg. One had been wounded there; another had been wounded near Richmond. One had been captured earlier in Maryland but had managed to escape just before being sent to Andersonville in Georgia.

"I heard other prisoners talking about how they was starving them damn prisoners to death down there. And they was either freezing in winter or burnin' up in summer. I knew that was not for me so I waited till I got a chance and I high tailed it out of camp one night. They shot at me but missed and I jest made up my mind to keep runnin' till another Reb bunch got me or I got to our boys. I made it to an Ohio regiment after a few hours. They was camped near to Gettysburg, still lickin' their wounds."

The fourth one said he had fought at Gettysburg with Colonel Joshua Chamberlain with the 20th Maine. That sounded vaguely familiar to Josh.

"Damn, you was the heroes of the whole battle," said one of the others. "As I hear tell, if it weren't for that bunch, on the second day, Lee would have flanked the Union main line and would have sent General Meade's whole corps skedaddlin' all over hell's half acre."

"You boys is gonna be remembered for a many a year for that bayonet charge," said the boy who had a long, threadlike mustache and sideburns. "Was that really true? We heard you was out of powder and bullets."

The "hero" just shrugged and said, "Let me tell ya, I was plenty scared as we formed up and charged down that hill from one side to the other. We was all screamin' like them damn Rebels do when they charge, but truth be known, I'd have to say I was screamin' just as much 'cuz I was scared to death. We didn't have no rounds left in our rifles is why we charged to begin with. We couldn't have withstood another Rebel attack on our position, so Colonel Chamberlain figured maybe we could catch 'em off guard and that's what we done with a bayonet charge. I done killed them Rebs before but shootin' them from a distance is different than stickin' 'em with a bayonet! The one I got was just as scared as me. If his musket hadn't misfired, I'd be in that cemetery over there today," he said as he gestured off to the side of the wagon as if the cemetery was right next to them, which in fact it was.

"I was sick to my stomach after I gave him the bayonet. He just looked at me in surprise, grabbed my gun barrel, and dropped right there. I had to let go my rifle as the bayonet and barrel went down with him. I couldn't bring myself to pull out the blade so I picked up his musket. I figured I'd also have a loaded rife then, but you know what? It looked like he had loaded it several times without knowin' it had misfired. Thing was all jammed up with powder and mine balls. I guess in the mix of the firing and killing, he just didn't realize what was happenin'. I just held it and ran down the hill with the rest of my company."

Josh listened intently to this as though it was story time or something. He felt astounded. He knew the 20th Maine sounded familiar and now he remembered the story from the battlefield guide when his family had gone to Gettysburg. It came back to him now like a rush. The guide had showed them in the woods where Colonel Chamberlain had ordered his men to charge, knowing they could not withstand another Rebel assault because they were so low on ammunition. This colonel, he remembered, was a college professor in Maine with no military experience before the war. He also remembered that he won the Medal of Honor for his actions that day as he apparently saved Meade from a disaster that could have changed the tide of the battle, the war, and thus even the United States.

Suddenly, as if on cue, they all looked at Josh and one started to ask a question, when the driver abruptly stopped the wagon in front of a large and stately residence in town. Josh had been so enthralled in listening to these young men that he hadn't noticed they had entered the town of Gettysburg, Pennsylvania.

"This here is the Wills House, where I'm supposed to drop you," he said as he motioned them to get down. "You are to join the rest of the boys and find the officer in charge. He'll tell you what to do. This here honor guard is made up of boys from all over the place." As they jumped down, Josh gave a huge sigh of relief that he had not had to try and explain what his part in this war was!

The driver pulled the reins to turn the horse and looked back at them. " I'm 'bout as sick of this war as a man can be, but I admire your courage, all of you. Hope you'll be back home with your families soon," he said and rode off.

They all looked around to get their bearings. Before they could decide which way to go, a short, stocky sergeant with reddish hair and blue eyes called them to fall in to a formation with a number of other boys and for the next hour they were given instructions as to what to do. Josh realized these soldiers were there mostly for show and as a reward for jobs well done in battle. The town square adjacent to the Wills House was filling up with people. The sergeant had told them that this was where Abraham Lincoln had spent the night. He instructed them to stand in rows of twos in the square, and in a matter of minutes, Josh noticed a flurry of activity and then saw this tall, thin, dark-haired man with the familiar beard and dark soulful eyes striding towards them.

This is a dream within a nightmare, thought Josh as he watched Mr. Lincoln in conversation with several men. Josh was almost overcome by all of this and had to take deep breaths to ward off a feeling of such weakness in his legs that he thought he might literally crumble. This was arguably the most renowned leader in the history of the United States, if not the world, and he was only a matter of a few yards away from Josh. His skin was rough and his face craggy, like someone who needed a vacation or was overtired. He mounted a horse with ease, looking a bit too big for it actually. He was dressed in a white shirt and black trousers, coat, shoes and looked warm as the day was headed towards a typical fall Indian summer day. The almost clichéd top hat was indeed perched on his head.

As he was forming with the procession, Lincoln guided his horse to within a few yards of where Josh and the guard company stood and gazed intently across the faces of the young men before him. He removed his hat and bowed his head slightly towards them with the trace of a smile in an unmistakable salute to his young troops.

"You boys, soldiers to a man, are the best hope we have as a country. I am doing my best to end this awful war and get you back to your homes and families in one piece. For those comrades you have lost, I apologize to you while having to say many more will no doubt be lost before it is all over. But you and I, we do what we have to to save this Union."

There was silence for a few seconds as he replaced his top hat on his large head. Then at once, a huge shout went up in the ranks, which was quickly, but gently, subdued by the several officers on horseback. Lincoln then turned his horse and walked him between two middle-aged gentlemen who Josh did not recognize and within minutes a grand military and civic procession began its way to the new cemetery. Josh now knew what this was all about. It was the dedication of the cemetery at Gettsyburg, where Mr. Lincoln would deliver a short address that would be as unforgettable as the man himself.

The procession to the cemetery moved from the square down Baltimore Street, passing numerous buildings and small intersections of streets. The honor guard of which Josh was now a temporary member moved out into the parade. Josh noticed many people waving from their doors and windows as the president's procession slowly worked its way toward the Gettysburg battlefield and the cemetery. They reached the entrance to the cemetery, an area that had obviously taken a beating from the Confederate artillery in preparation for Pickett's charge and the final climax of the three day battle. Josh noticed with amazement that ironically there was a sign posted that read, "All persons found using firearms on these grounds will be prosecuted with the utmost rigor of the law."

As Josh looked around, he could see signs of the battle everywhere. There were pieces of wagons, marred and broken trees and fences, and discarded canteens. This after almost six months had elapsed since the actual battle had been fought, in which there were at least 50,000 Union and Confederate American casualties combined. Josh was getting that panicky feeling again that he had experienced at other times when he was caught up in these strange historical flashbacks, not knowing what to expect or what to do. A man who introduced himself as Mr. Edward Everett, who was the main speaker of the day, was droning on and on. Josh could feel the sweat under his arms and down the small of his back as he felt he might have to bolt, when suddenly Everett finished to polite applause. Mr. Lincoln was then immediately introduced and Josh was suddenly calmer. He felt as though he was watching a movie. And then he began to hear those words he had read so many times before—words that were usually part of an assignment to memorize from a history book or in some documentary. Now suddenly, through this weird flashback of which he had not the slightest understanding nor could he explain, he heard them as if they were spoken for the first time.

> "Four score and seven years ago.... dedicated to the proposition that all men are created equal. We have come to dedicate a portion of that field....we cannot consecrate this ground...The brave men living and dead....consecrated it far above our poor power to add or detract... these dead shall not have died in vain.... that this nation, under God, shall have a new birth of freedom-and that government of the people, by the people, for the people, shall not perish from the earth."

The unforgettable words were still ringing in his ears from the tall, lanky, weary-looking man who had removed his famous top hat, when the applause from the crowd swept over them as he and the rest of the honor guard watched. He tried to focus on all that was happening—especially Lincoln, as he shook hands with a number of people as he turned from the podium. A speech, so remarkable because it delivered a potent message for today and for the ages, and yet was only minutes in length. With that thought, he began to feel very tired and lightheaded.

CHAPTER XI
Doubts

It was really his room. He felt so good under the covers. The clean smell of the detergent his mom used to wash the sheets and pillow cases filled his nostrils as he lay there collecting his thoughts. *Shit!* It had happened again. Just when he thought maybe this whole thing of flashbacks might be over, he had suddenly been transported back in time to an honor guard for Abraham Lincoln. *That's right! Not just any person from those stormy days, but arguably the most famous president in our history as he gave one of the most famous addresses ever heard. But so what!!!!* he thought. *Not to downplay the event's importance, but what does it all have to do with Josh Gershwin and what the hell am I supposed to make of all this? Jeez, I gotta get a grip,* he thought. He checked his watch. Nine o'clock.

He quickly jumped out of bed and lightly padded down the hall to see if his parents were still asleep, which would be typical for a Sunday. After all they were Jewish, so Saturday, not Sunday, was their Sabbath. Not that they were big temple goers, but in any event Sunday was usually a sleep-in day. He felt a sigh of relief as he saw them both still asleep. These flashbacks were so confusing and seemed so real that he just couldn't fathom what was actually happening. He assumed his body was to all appearances asleep during these episodes…but…but what if it wasn't? What if he were physically gone! No way. It had to be a mind thing, but still he wondered. Well so far, at least, he had no indication that it was anything other than some form of dream and/or daze. When it came over him as in a daze, he wasn't really unconscious but his mind was somewhere else and he had no awareness of the present.

During his episode in class, he was actually awake and acting out the flashback. That in itself was a really scary thought. What if he suddenly had a flashback to Picket's Charge or something like that in the middle of a shopping mall, or a movie? Who knows what antics he might pull off!! He could get arrested! Also what, if anything, was the relationship of his dad's Springfield rifle to these bizarre happenings? As he mulled over this, he realized that in every occurrence the rifle was there and/or was in his thoughts either before or afterwards. Returning to his room, he laid down again and picked up a rubber band off of his nightstand and began pulling and twisting it while he stared at the ceiling, trying to figure some things out.

This business of being a part-time Civil War soldier was going to drive him crazy. Was he in danger while on these little "trips"? Were these simply very realistic dreams? If so, how did he get that bruise he had from his earlier episode? Had it come from thrashing around while unconscious? He preferred that explanation. Should he tell his parents what was happening? Would they want him to go to a shrink? Probably. At one time he would not have entertained that for even a second. He was still not ready to go to his parents, but it took him several minutes of pros and cons thinking to arrive at that decision. He wasn't ready yet.

As for Penny, what now? This past week was definitely the lowest point in the relatively short time he had known her. He had tried to engage her any number of times in homeroom, during class, after class, before class, you name it. He even followed her to the girl's bathroom and waited outside for her. That was one of his more idiotic moves. His mind replayed the event.

She emerged with two of her friends, who got a big kick out of his being there. "Well, look who is here just waiting for you to finish up in the ladies' room," said Sharon, smiling as she eyed Josh very slowly from head to toe. Susan, the other one, didn't really acknowledge his existence but she definitely rubbed against him as she pushed passed him. She had very large boobs and she always tried to accentuate them. In this case, if they had been two paint rollers, Josh's shirt would have looked like a freshly painted canvas.

Feeling pretty ridiculous, Josh just smiled sheepishly at Penny and said, "Could I have a word with you, Penny?"

"I'm sorry, Josh," said Penny with a nod to the two girls to keep moving. "I'm really in a hurry right now, as we're going to be late getting to the cafeteria for lunch."

"Oh, hey I know ze maitre de," he said in his best French accent. "I can get you zeated nooh problem." Sharon and Susan laughed out loud but Penny pressed on without making direct eye contact. "Thanks Josh, but I gotta go." And with that she sped away and he was alone. As he looked up, the bathroom door opened again and Mrs. Sutton walked out. "Can I help you, Josh?" she asked, obviously wondering what he was doing standing right in front of the girls' bathroom door.

"Uh no, Mrs. Sutton, I was just, um, getting ready to go have lunch," he said, wishing immediately that he could take that back. He blushed.

She blushed too! Shaking her head, she pointed towards the cafeteria. "Just a guess Josh, but I think today's lunch specials are in there."

Actually, she knew he had a crush on Penny and that it was not going well and when she saw him, she figured he had been waiting for Penny. Teachers knew a lot more than their students gave them credit for; and in addition, she had seen Penny and her friends primping at the mirror a few minutes ago.

Josh focused on the pointing finger and turned, immediately heading for the cafeteria.

"Absolutely, Mrs. Sutton, see you later."

Christ, she reduces me to an idiot every time, he thought as he meandered in the direction of the cafeteria, not feeling particularly hungry. Well, Penny had certainly cooled his heels. She could either be fine with her decision, giving him the cold shoulder to make sure he got the message, or she could be struggling inside and trying to keep her distance from him so as not to give in to his good looks and terrific personality! He smiled at his self- description! It was obviously the latter!

Penny sat down at the cafeteria table with her tray and eyed her two friends suspiciously. The full up-and-down scrutiny that Sharon had given Josh and the boob power play of Susan did not go unnoticed by Penny. She suspected that her friends were actually jealous of Josh's feelings for her. Feeling the coldness of her stare, Sharon said, "I get the feeling we're in trouble, Susan," and with that she looked at Susan and shrugged her most innocent shrug.

"For whatever reason would that be," Susan said, turning her most innocent gaze toward Penny.

"Look you two, I'm not blind. Between the two of you, Josh could file charges for sexual molestation, for Christ's sake. Here I am trying my damnedest to forget about him and you two act like two dogs in heat."

"Now wait a minute, *Miss I'm goin' to college and don't wanna have anything to do with Josh Gershwin!!*"

"I'm sorry, Sharon" Penny said as she played with her spaghetti. "It's just that in spite of what I told you, I'm really struggling with this thing and to have you two practically drooling over him right in front of me doesn't help."

"Well, I wouldn't call it drooling exactly," Susan said as she coolly stuck her fork in a round little tomato in her salad and popped it into her mouth.

"Really," said Penny, half smiling with a napkin to her mouth.

"If your boobs had prints like fingers, you could be identified just from Josh's shirt! And you, Sharon, what exactly were you looking for as you scanned him from head to toe. Did you find it?" She arched a dark, perfect eyebrow. "Were you trying to discover something along the way?"

"Well, you know, he is Jewish, and, uh, you know, they are all, uh…you know…"

"Are you referring to circumcision, Sharon?" Penny asked as her eyes darted left then right and then back on Sharon. "Most boys are circumcised today you know, regardless of religion."

"Yeah, but with Jews, you know for sure—some kind of pact between them and God. Part of their culture." Sharon lowered her voice to a whisper. "Penny, have you seen his…"

Before she could finish her sentence, Penny emptied her milk carton on Sharon's plate, causing the meat sauce to look more like tomato soup.

"I'm not even going to dignify that with an answer, Sharon," Penny said, with her face turning crimson.

"Oh, dignity! Yes very dignified *you* are," Sharon said as she watched her spaghetti floating in the white liquid and saw Susan trying to get a sauce stain off one of her boobs that had been splashed when Penny poured the milk.

"Besides, I was just going to say… his, uh, silver Bar Mitzvah cup, they all get them you know. It's part of the ceremony when they have to say a prayer and sip wine."

"And I suppose you thought he had it hidden somewhere in his pants, huh?"

With that Penny looked at Susan and they both rolled their eyes and laughed.

"Sure you were, Sharon. How do you know about Jewish Bar Mitzvah customs anyway?" Penny asked, the anger gone from her tone now.

"I've been to a couple of them in the past few years. Brothers of some Jewish friends I have," Sharon replied.

"Listen," Penny said. "Just don't make matters worse for me is all I ask. Last night I lay in bed not able to sleep, thinking about how good it felt when he danced close with me at Sam's and how warm his lips were when we kissed. Uh, well, actually I should say when *he* kissed *me*."

Sharon and Susan exchanged looks that didn't need words. "Now *who is bullshitting who?*" Sharon thundered. Penny just sighed and shrugged her shoulders. They all rose from their seats to head to homeroom before next class.

As they went through the oak and glass doors into the hall, Susan said *see you later* with a wave and headed off. Sharon turned to Penny with a somber (at least for Sharon) look and said, "You know Penny, if I wasn't worried about the interfaith thing with my family, I would be putting myself right out there, encouraging him to ask me out since you've said you're not interested anymore. Maybe someday in the future it won't be as big a deal, but at this point in time, I've been raised as a staunch Baptist and it's too big a mountain for me to climb right now. He's a good guy—funny, sexy, good looking, smart, and sophisticated. At least sophisticated for a boy of seventeen, anyway. He does behave a little weird on occasion," she said, thinking of the North versus the South classroom antics a while back, "but at least it's funny and not hurtful or redneck city like so many of these adolescent boys."

"I know," Penny said, lowering her head and noticing what looked like spilled milk on her navy blue shoes. "Well, until now I never had any doubts about how I would handle this kind of a situation before graduating high school and going to college. The irony is I'm not that concerned over the interfaith thing, but I know my parents would be and that would be trouble. You and my parents," Penny forced a bit of a laugh. "Well, at least I don't have to worry about you trying to take him, should I change my mind, huh?"

"Well, no probably not, but I don't think you can take much comfort in that," Sharon said as she looked past Penny to see Josh walking up the stairs and four girls not far behind him, giggling and pointing to his handsomely shaped butt. "I probably won't be your problem, but they may be."

Penny turned and saw the same view, except at that moment Josh must have heard the giggling and looked back down the steps and his eyes met Penny's. He started to smile, but walking upstairs while looking backwards was not one of his strong points and he tripped on the step and had to grab the hand rail. That made his fan club behind him howl with laughter as only adolescent girls can. Too embarrassed to look back, he rounded the stairwell. Penny just sighed and nodded to Sharon as they headed to their homeroom.

CHAPTER XII
Jingle Bells 'n Musket Shells

The days melted away and soon it was almost Christmas—that time of year known for its joy and merriment—and this year it was returning to the normal, celebratory feel. The previous year, Christmas was a dark time for the country, with Kennedy having just been assassinated. Now it was late 1964 and Richmond, like most of America, was emerging from the Kennedy assassination horror and the sort of funk that followed it.

There was a new hope and optimism in the youth of the country, replacing a sort of malaise that had been apparent for the past year. The optimism was brought on by time elapsed from the tragedy, for one thing, but also by a general feeling in the country that things were going to get better. A certain vibrancy was palpable in the youth of America. A young, cocky and brilliant fighter named Cassius Clay had astounded the world by taking the heavyweight championship away from Sonny Liston in February and on the heels of that feat, a certain British group called the Beatles landed in America.

Rock and Roll had seized the country in the 50's, giving the post-WWII generation a much needed self identity, but it had been floundering with folk music, moving into the vacuum. Rock, the once great love of teens, seemed to have no direction or link to anything meaningful. Suddenly Beatlemania washed over America's shores, taking the nation by storm. Having swept Britain the year before with all its fresh sounds, new culture, new clothes, increased sexual freedom and long hair, it was now blossoming in the U.S., and with it, a sort of subculture that was growing stronger every day.

The Beatles were probably the first pop artists who talked to the press as equals with wit and intelligence. At any rate, it was a time of better feelings in the country and it was a boost America needed, along with most Western European countries, Australia, Canada, and on and on. Suddenly the world was a little smaller and friendlier place if you were among the youth of the day.

Josh awoke on Tuesday, December 15, as his clock radio came on with the sounds of the Beach Boys' "Little St. Nick." It was that time of year again, and Jewish or not, Josh really enjoyed it. There was something about Christmas and this time of year that just got to him. It was obviously not a religious thing, but it was a spiritual thing of sorts in that it lifted his spirits. The festive atmosphere all over school was good for him as he was down because Penny was still ignoring him and he was still having these Civil War flashbacks.

In the past month and a half, he had had three more flashbacks. They were in no particular chronological order, he noticed, but seemed to be just random. In the last one he was at a battle in Manassas in 1862, which he knew was referred to as the second Manassas (the first one having occurred in 1861 and was considered the first real battle of the war). He knew this from history class but also because as he was running with the rest of the young men in blue as fast as they could, ducking and dodging minet balls he heard one of them yell.

"God Damn it, this here's second time we done been run out of this Manassas town in less than two years. Last time we ran clear cross the Potomac and didn't stop till we got to Washington!!"

Josh had definitely not been in any mood to run 20 miles or whatever the hell it was from northern Virginia across the Potomac to Washington, D.C., so he looked for somewhere to go to escape the fleeing mob. To his left he caught site of a stream (which he later figured out must have been Bull Run—another name for these two battles) and he feigned tripping and fell off to the side. He needn't have tried to hide it because no one noticed as they all ran for their lives with the Rebels advancing in their rear, throwing shot and shell at them, which, luckily, was going high and over their heads at this point.

He rolled several yards and more down the embankment, letting his musket go in the thick grass as he slid in into the shallow water, dropping to his knees. He welcomed the cool sensation. It was a hot, humid, August Virginia day. Amidst all of the smoke and noise of artillery, it felt safe to be in the water. He crawled to a place that was hidden by tree limbs and leaves and just relaxed, lying propped up against a fallen tree in the water and let the war just pass by, literally.

Suddenly, Josh had the feeling he was not alone. He froze in the water, dropping down so that only his head was above the surface. He looked through the maze of branches and leaves around him and realized that he was face to face with and only a couple yards from a soldier, who must have had the same idea. He was also down in the water so that only his head protruded.

As he sat on the bed in his room, this morning, he couldn't help but relive the scene as it was so vivid in his memory.

He had looked at the young man, guessing he was no more than eighteen. "Hello! My name is Josh, Josh Gershwin," Josh heard himself say. "I'm from Richmond, Virginia. Nice to meet you," he said.

"Hey. I'm Charles Parcel; nice to meet you, too," the teenager said. "I'm from a little hamlet in western Virginia."

The accent was a lot like some of the kids he went to school with actually, thought Josh, except it had this faint touch of something else in it. British maybe. *A southern hick with a touch of the Brits in him?* He was about to ask him what the hell they were going to do now, when he noticed Charles' eyes go wide and fearful as he stared at the top of Josh's head. Josh instinctively looked up at Charles' head and suddenly was gripped with a cold fear as well. Charles wore a gray cap! A Confederate cap!

That's what Charles was staring at: Josh's dark blue Union cap. Josh looked to see if his rifle was nearby (which would have been worth little more than a club, as he still had never loaded or fired it). It was on the bank a good twenty yards away. He had a bayonet on his belt, which he quickly put his right hand upon, ready to yank it out if necessary.

Charles, in the mean time, was in a similar situation. Not wanting to get his rifle wet, he had tossed it on the bank as well. He did not have his bayonet, having lost it some time ago, but he had a small pocket knife, which he now hurriedly fished for underwater.

Josh came up with his bayonet first, trying to get some feel for how to hold this thing which had no handle. Charles moved backward in the water, still staying low to keep himself covered, and brought up his pocket knife, which opened to about a three-inch blade.

There they were, two heads and two hands above the surface of the water, glaring at each other—one with the little knife, the other with a foot-long bayonet wobbling around in his hand. After staring frozen in fear for a few moments, they began to relax a bit. Josh spoke first.

"Hey, I don't want to do you any harm, my friend. I'm not even supposed to be here, but that's too long a story right now," he said as he opened his hand and let the silver heavy bayonet lay balanced across his palm.

Charles, the Confederate, looked relieved and did the same with his knife, laying it in the palm of his hand.

"Hey, I'm new to this here war," he said. "This here's the first action I ever seen, and ta tell you the truth, it ain't what them damn scoundrels told me—them that convinced me to join up."

"Well," Josh said, "First things first." He tossed his bayonet some twenty to thirty feet into the middle of the stream. Charles stared at the splash for a few seconds and then tossed his knife into the same region.

"Whew… I'm glad we done got that over with. I don't really wanna keel nobody and ain't fixin' to die myself right about now."

"How old are you?" Josh asked him.

"I'm jest turned seventeen. Been farmin' fer my family all ma life. Anxious to get back to it, too. Had 'nuff of this here solderin'. Can't git no decent food nor clothes and don't believe in this here southern cause no how. Them black folk, they ain't deservin' to be sold off an' fam'lies split up like they is. We never had no slaves in my family. Pa don't believe in it."

Josh was startled by this boy's honesty and sensitivity to the slaves' plight. Not that he was any expert on it.

Two hours later, the two boys had pulled themselves onto the bank and removed their shirts to dry off. Josh shared his rations with Charles, who ate like he was nearly starved, which he was. Josh could count nearly every rib.

He was wearing a homemade kind of outfit that was a sort of gray beige and was full of tears and holes. It was almost evening by now, shadows were long and the sun was sinking behind the trees. Josh tried for the first time ever to explain his situation to someone participating in his flashbacks: That he was not really here but having flashbacks from a point about a hundred years in the future. He said he would be going back there soon.

He couldn't quite get through to Charles, who just sort of shook his head each time Josh tried to explain. Since Josh didn't know what the hell was really happening either, it was fairly impossible to not sound loony. Charles just understood him to be saying he came from a long way off and was going home soon.

The battle had long since ended. It was so quiet you could hear the stream gurgling. "Charles, did you have to do any fighting today?" inquired Josh as he played with a piece of hard tack that was truly hard as a brick.

"Yes suh, I did," Charles said matter-of-factly without a trace of ego or pride. "My company was part of an attack 'long some railway cuts that ain't got no tracks yet. We laid in to yer boys pretty hard. I know'd I shot at least two, maybe more. Not something I wanted to do but had no choice. My sergeant was watchin' me and I know'd he'd a shot me if I hadn't gotten in the middle. One of them boys was only a few yards away and I saw him wince as my minie ball hit him in the side. He went down like he'd been hit by a two by four. Just fell into the middle of them boys and disappeared into a mess o' runnin' legs n' boots and churned up grass."

Josh could hear his voice was choked with emotion. "I shot anothern when we wuz runnin' along chasin' you boys. I looked up and saw one of them turnin' and rasin' his musket and he was looking right at *me* as he sighted down the barrel! I dropped to the ground jest as he fired and ya know, I heard that there ball whistle right by my ear as I was fallin'. Soon's I hit the ground I didn't even think, I jest raised up my rifle while he was tryin' to reload and I shot at him.

"I guess I'm a pretty good shot, been shootin' round the farm since I's a little youngin'. I think I hit him in the shoulder. It spun him clean round. He had a blank stare on his face as he reached up with his other arm and grabbed at the pain. Then he jest sort a dropped like somebody done pulled a rug out from under him. They was yellin' at us to keep after you boys so I didn't even get to stop and see if he was dead or livin'. But he wasn't movin' when I ran by him and he was pale…Josh, he was so pale…I don't think he was no older then me." He stared off for a minute, obviously overcome by what he was saying he had done. Then he composed himself a bit.

"Must a been 'bout a mile or more from here. We chased you Yankees that far, I reckon. I tell ya, Josh, we must have been in five or six different actions yesterday and today. Our division was just plum wore out. Ya know, I kept telling myself it wasn't like I was a-murderin' nobody…they'd a shot *me* if'n I hadn't fired first. I asked God if he would think of it that way too but course I didn't git no answer. Guess I'll find out one day when it's my turn ta go. Ya know, where I wind up, I mean."

"Yes, I know," Josh said as he tried to will himself out of this dream or nightmare or whatever it was.

"Well, I guess I'm gonna git," Charles said as he stood up and put his raggedy shirt on. "I'm not goin' back to my company. I'm goin' home. Like I said. I jest had 'nuff. Probly take me weeks to get there, if I don't get rounded up as a deserter or shot by one of you blue-dressed fellers. I'll travel at night and sleep durin' the day. It was nice to meet you, Josh. You have a good trip to ,uh… wherever it is yer goin!"

With that, he picked up his musket, slung it over his shoulder and disappeared into the woods. Josh sat contemplating what he had seen and heard this day, and as he went over to find his rifle in the dusk, and he picked it up, he was thankful he had not had to endure or witness any of the fighting this time. It was a sight no one should have to see. In fact Josh had read that with all the hundreds of civil war photographs by Mathew Brady and his associates, not one depicts a view during the actual fighting. Probably because of the danger and because you had to pose absolutely still for the image to not be blurry. Yet it seemed to Josh it was almost as if, you had to earn the right to see the battle, by having been there. Well Josh had been there too often and was ready to get back home, now.

He remembered now, sitting in his room how that evening he had sat by that creek thinking how the weapons they were using were too advanced for their tactics, causing mass casualties as they just stood in lines facing or walking directly at one another. And that was loading and firing rifles one bullet at a time. Imagine if they had repeating rifles or machine guns. Only Cavalry typically had any repeaters, not the infantry; and gattling guns were still being perfected and not in much use. The canister shot was the worst. As his mind raced back to some of the vivid and horrid scenes he had witnessed, he had suddenly felt a chill and his eyes had grown heavy.

He remembered hearing an angry voice but it trailed off as he had drifted off. That is until, as had become the norm, he had awakened safe in his home. This time he had been sitting in the chair in the den, which was where he had been sitting when he began that "voyage"! It did not appear as though he moved around when in this trance, dream, or whatever it was. He still wondered if his dad's rifle was the cause of these flashbacks and though he did not have one every time he came into contact with it, it was usually in close proximity or he had very recently been near it. The only flashback he suffered through while not close to the rifle was the one at school when Mr. Pelter was talking to the school over the class speaker system. It was still a mystery for sure.

CHAPTER XIII
Questioning

Chanukah was a sort of nonevent at Josh's house. They lit the candles and gave a small present on each of the eight days but it wasn't a big religious holiday with the stature of Yom Kippur or Rosh Hashanah or even Passover. Truth be known, Josh always suspected it was just a small celebration that grew in stature because of its proximity to Christmas. As the impact of Christmas grew in Europe and America through the ages, so then it seemed had Chanukah, at least for some. Now of course the whole world seemed to be singing and decorating, excited about Christmas. There was a feeling in the air that was hard to ignore, irrespective of a person's religion. Josh really enjoyed the Christmas spirit and made no excuses. The deejay at WLIE came on and promised this December 16th was going to be a chilly day after a very cold night. The daytime high would only reach 41 degrees; currently, early morning temperature was a very cold 25. That was a bit colder than normal for Richmond. The long-term projection for those hoping for a white Christmas was not good, though. Warmer than usual air was headed for Virginia on Christmas day. It could bring temperatures in the sixties, according to the station's weather guy. *Well, what the hell, snow would have been a nice change,* but Josh thought, *no big deal.*

In another week or so, he would be off for the holidays but there was so much going on right now. He had to contend with a heavy load at school, for one thing. He just completed and turned in a term paper for English literature, which was a ball buster. The usual tests and heavy homework load were certainly laid on before the holidays.

As he lay there with all these thoughts running through his head, he suddenly found himself thinking about that stupid flashback again. He tried not to dwell on these damn incidents but something was not sitting right with him. Something kept going round in his head… Something familiar yet odd and he tried to put his finger on it…and then it hit him! The young soldier he had had the encounter with in the water, uh….Parcel….Charles Parcel…. That name sounded awful familiar—but why? He wasn't sure but something about it was definitely rolling around in his head.

He got dressed for school. It was last day before the holidays and he was able to borrow the car from his mother with the legitimate excuse that he needed to go to the public library after school. He did, in fact, need to go to the library though it wasn't going to be for school! Actually, at this point, he wasn't sure what he was going to be looking for other than that name had to have some significance. All day he kept going over the flashback to Manassas, trying to picture Charles and trying to connect the name. Suddenly he remembered where he thought he had heard it before. *It can't be!*

He made it a point to find Penny at lunch as he had to ask her an important question. He knew she wasn't talking to him officially, but he still felt she was interested in him. On occasion he would catch her eying him or overdoing the "I don't care" bit when other girls flirted with him, but she remained true to her word in that she barely spoke to him other than a brief nod or slight wave if he waved first.

He caught up with her in the cafeteria as she was getting ready to sit with some of her friends, including Sharon and Susan.

"Hey, Ms. Collingsly, I really need a few moments of your time," he said, trying to be nonchalant but looking her directly in the eye.

"Oh Josh, I'm famished and I need to get back to my homeroom so I'm in a rush to gobble this stuff down," she said, still standing as she averted his gaze and looked down to her seated friends. When she looked back at him she sort of focused on his mouth and not his eyes as she spoke. "Besides, I don't think we have that much to talk about anyway, at this point," she said coldly.

"Listen to me, Penny," Josh said as he moved to face her directly. "I have a few things I need to ask you about. I'm not trying to get you to go out with me or anything like that. I know it's over between us. I wonder now even if there was really that much there to begin with." And with that he moved off to an empty table, two tables over from hers. He sat and he waited, not looking at her. He didn't mean the last comment at all. He was as bound up with feelings for her as he ever was but he suddenly had realized it was time he tested the resilience of her decision. And besides, he honestly did want to ask her some questions related to doing some research on this latest flashback.

Penny stood silent for a few seconds, her mind racing. She had been determined to end whatever it was they had, because she knew it had the potential to become serious. She had ended it for the right reasons (school focus and different religions with all their family overtones). She had somehow just figured he would get over the hurt *but not really get over her!* This was her first realization that maybe she could not count on that. In these few seconds, reality struck. The color drained from her cheeks, her legs felt weak, and she felt her eyes beginning to brim with tears.

She quickly turned so her friends could not see her tears and said loudly, enough for them to hear while looking in Josh's direction, "Okay, I forgot to get a napkin; I'll be there in a second."

Josh had looked away when he sat down, so he didn't see the emotion she was trying hard to hide or the two napkins already on her tray. Sharon and Susan saw it all. They looked at each other and Sharon's eyes rolled up as she shook her head.

As Penny headed toward the condiments table, Sharon said, "Christ! I have dreams about dancing slow with him and feeling his lips on mine and his arms around me. He's definitely a turn on. Not to mention that butt! Being Jewish is part of his charm, I think. At one point I convinced myself that dating him just for fun would be …uh….well…you know…fun and all right!!! Nothing serious so the Baptist guilt thing wouldn't have to be dealt with, but I've been a faithful friend to her and have not come on to him or anything. Not that it would have phased him any. But now she'll have to deal with reality, huh? He may be actually losing interest in her at last. Her little game of wanting it both ways is falling apart and she's just realizing it now.

"I can't believe it took him this long to set her straight," she continued. "It just shows how much class he has…he's been dedicated to her since October without any response. She's my best friend and I love her dearly, but she's been living in a dream world and no matter what I told her she wouldn't listen."

Susan, a girl of few words, just nodded as she watched Penny quickly touch the new napkin to her eyes and head for Josh's table. She usually found herself at odds with Sharon's posturing about such things but she could not argue on this one. Although she thought Josh was still smitten, she had to admit it appeared cracks in the foundation were beginning to show.

Penny walked directly to Josh's table, collecting herself to hide the emotions that a minute ago had been so near the surface. She sat down next to him. "Hi, Josh. Sorry I was so short with you back there." She tried to weed out any emotion from her voice. "What's up?" she asked, a bit too cheerily.

Josh started to say something but just held it for a minute while he looked at her. *She is feeling something,* he thought. *There is no question about it.* He saw the beginning of a tear in the corner of her eye. He could wait her out here as he felt she was going to break down, but he did not want to embarrass her and certainly not in this place, so he quickly opened his notebook and said, "Hey, this is going to sound really weird, but I need some information about your family. Like a bit of their history."

She had a lump in her throat that she had to get by first before she could speak. She could tell he was aware of her emotion at that point and had spared her. He could have been cruel and really hurt and embarrassed her as she was on the verge of breaking down. This is why she could not shake her feelings for this boy, no matter how much she had tried. This was why she wept alone in her bedroom when no one could see. Why she would stand in the shower in the morning with the water pouring over her body, thinking of him and how much he meant to her.

But each day, by the time she arrived at school, she would talk herself into the belief that her feelings for him were okay as long as she just didn't act on them and stayed true to her focus on academics and college. More than once she had questioned herself as to whether that really was the reason. Or was she just scared of the kind of feelings he stirred in her?

She realized he was writing some notes and waiting for her to "resurface." She was so thankful for a reprieve and something different to think and talk about that she didn't even question why he wanted the information about her family. This was good because Josh, in his haste, had not for a minute considered what he would say if she asked him why he wanted to know. He wasn't ready to share his thoughts in that direction yet.

"So you want to know some of my family history?"

"Yeah, mainly on background of your parents. If you'll humor me for now, I will tell you why later."

Not wanting to change the subject, Penny said, "Well my grandfather, Michael Collingsly, came to the U.S. from Ireland around 1900 as a young ambitious man. He came into New York and by chance wound up settling in the western part of Virginia. He opened a general dry goods store, so the story goes, and made a pretty good success of it. He met and married my grandmother soon after and then my dad Michael Jr. was born, not long after. Not much to tell there. Just the normal American immigrants who worked hard to make a place for themselves."

"And your mother," Josh said, feeling a tingling in his foot.

"Well, that's a more involved story," she said, checking the clock and throwing a quick glance to her friends. She was relieved to see that they were gone.

"My great great great grandfather, on my mom's side, Charles, came to the United States in his twenties from a town near London around 1840, already married to my great great great grandmother, Emma. They came into Baltimore and then traveled to the western part of Virginia to settle. He had enough money from his sale of a small farm in England to buy some property here and begin another one. He just wanted to live in the mountains in America and he heard

Virginia was the most beautiful place there was. At least that is how the story goes. He only had one son, my great great grandfather Charles Jr. He was born in 1845 on the farm in Virginia."

A chill passed over Josh as he did the math in his head. *Born in 1845…that would make him seventeen in 1862 at the Battle of Manassas.* That was what *Charles* had said his age was when Josh asked him in his flashback. Thinking further, he quickly figured that if this line of her ancestors had their offspring in their mid-twenties to thirties, her dad could easily be in his mid-fifties today.

"Just two more questions," he said. "What is your mom's age and her maiden name?"

"Hmm, my mom is 44 and her maiden name is Parcel." Josh felt a shiver down his spine. It gave him goose bumps! In fact, it gave his goose bumps their own goose bumps!

He got up and smiled and nodded to her as he walked toward the cafeteria doors. "Josh!" Penny called out. He stopped and turned toward her. "Promise you'll fill me in on what this is about later?" she asked. She wanted to say more but decided now was not the time; she felt too vulnerable.

"I will do that," he replied as he turned and pushed through the doors into the hall.

She sat alone playing with her food, but not eating till next bell rang.

By the time Josh got to the library after school, he had a plan in his mind to do the research. It took him some time to find an open meter to park downtown near the library but he filled it with as much change as it would allow and bounded up the steps into the old building. He wondered if there would be any holiday grace given by the police if he forgot to come out and put money in the meter, which had been wrapped so nicely in green fir and red ribbons. He concluded there would not.

The library was also warmly decorated with a tall tree and lights. It was probably typical of many libraries across the country in the sixties—built before any thoughts of branch libraries with massively tall ceilings and not much efficient use of space.

He found the research area and began to look for articles on the Civil War and specifically the second battle of Manassas. Some three and a half hours later, he was done. Having fed the meter several times in the interim, he had taken several pages of notes and he slowly approached his mom's car, shaking his head. This was more incredible then he could ever have imagined. In his research, with the help of the librarian, he followed a hunch that if there really was a Charles Parcel in the Confederate Army coming out of southwestern Virginia, he might well have been in the corps of the great General Stonewall Jackson, whose base of operations was usually in the Shenandoah Valley and Blue Ridge Mountains of Virginia.

First thing to research was whether or not Jackson and his division participated in the Second Manassas battle, since his flashback placed Charles there. In fact, Jackson's corps was a major part of it, Josh soon learned. Next, which commanders were under Jackson and could he get to their rosters? He was able to find the commanders under Jackson but that was all he could find. That's where the librarian came in. He asked for help from her and, not surprisingly, in Richmond during the 1960s Civil War centennial years, she proved to be knowledgeable about such matters, having answered many questions and looked for data of a similar nature many times. She was incredibly helpful. Josh wasn't about to explain the full reason behind his research; he just said it was the great great grandfather of his *girlfriend* (he wished) on whom he was looking for information. Josh never realized that this kind of research could be exciting, probably because he had never done any of it before that wasn't driven by a teacher telling him what the topic and events had to be.

Suddenly he was face to face with rosters of Jackson's corps divisions by commander, and there, under General A.P. Hill's division rosters, under Brigade Commander Dorsey Pender, in some very old dusty books, they found the name of one Corporal Charles Parcel Jr., who was age sixteen at enlistment. The spelling was the same as Penny's mother's maiden name.

They didn't have time to go into too many records beyond the roster search because it was getting late in the afternoon. Josh did read in one excerpt from Stonewall Jackson's own Manassas 1862 battle report submitted to Colonel Chilton, Inspector General that Hill reported that he made six different assaults which were all repulsed . This did tie in with Charles' own estimation that he had been in five or six actions at Manassas and was "plumb wore out."

He hadn't asked Penny about any Civil War history in her family because he remembered from their work on the project at school for Malvern Hill that, while she did know her family had some war connections, she didn't know any specifics. The librarian told him that armed with Parcel's rank and unit designation which he now had, he stood a good chance of getting more specific information from the National Archives in Washington. She gave him a form that he could fill out and mail. She said it was possible that he could get copies of Parcel's muster records attendance, battle wounds, special type awards, and more. Josh thought, *Nope, I got all I need.*

CHAPTER XIV
The Naked Truth

As he drove home from the library, Josh had mixed emotions. *What the hell did this mean? How could this have happened? How could he have had a flashback where he met Penny's mother's great grandfather as a seventeen-year-old kid at the Second Battle of Manassas? That was not only incredible, but it was downright scary as well. Who was pulling these strings!!!*

Assuming these flashbacks continued, would he meet Charles again? There was no telling because they came and went in no particular order. Gettysburg's cemetery dedication flashback was before this one, and yet chronologically in history, it was more than a year after the second Manassas. Maybe unconsciously he had heard Penny say her mother's maiden name and something about her ancestor being in the Civil War. He quickly dismissed that coincidence as he certainly would have remembered a story concerning her great great grandfather being at Manassas, including his name, his young age, and so forth. And he didn't believe for a minute that Penny even knew all that information. He could call her just to see if he had served in the military and it would also be a chance to talk to her again. He made up his mind. He would do it before dinner.

An hour later, his heart raced as he sat on his parents' bed and listened to the clickety-clack of the phone ringing Penny's number.

"Hello?" What luck, it was her!

"Hi, Penny. Josh here."

"Josh, it was good to talk to you today, it really was… but I'm—"

"Yeah, it was good to talk to you today, too; it's been ages."

There was silence on the other end. He knew she was thinking that he just couldn't resist calling her after having talked to her at school today. She wasn't ready to encourage him… yet. He was convinced deep down inside though, that it was only a matter of time and subtle perseverance. Maybe that was a wild leap on his part, but, hey, he did have some ego. Well, he wasn't going to let her think that he was desperate, and besides, he was calling for a reason.

"Actually, Penny, I need some more information regarding my questions at lunch today."

"Well, I was uh…I mean…I was going to say I just showered and I'm dripping wet in a towel. Can you call me back later, maybe?"

Hmmm, dripping wet in a towel…nice vision, Josh thought. Or maybe it was just a ruse to get off the phone with him quickly.

"Okay, just answer me one question and you can run, I promise," he said, trying to keep from thinking about her in that towel.

"Uh, okay Josh, what is the question?" she said hurriedly but with a slight softening of her tone, he thought.

"Was your maternal great great grandfather in the military? If so, when did he join?"

"That's two questions," she teased. "Actually, I think he was in the military but I'm not sure if it was the Civl War or the Spanish American and I don't have a clue how old he was when he joined."

"All right, that's fine," he said, thinking how sexy she must look in that towel and feeling himself getting flustered. "Well, I guess I'd better get you out of that wet towel…uh… I mean… I guess I *letter bet you* …uh…*better let you*…uh you know what I mean. I'll let you run, Penny." *Shit*…he thought. *That was not cool!* In fact that would have been embarrassing for some of the squares he knew at school and it's hard to embarrass those guys!

She was stifling a laugh, he could tell. "What's wrong Josh? Do all undressed girls dripping in towels get you tongue tied or just me?" She found it hard to resist a little flirting.

He was silent for a moment. He could feel his face getting hot. Thankfully they were on the phone and his blushing was not visible.

"Penny, I, uh… You know it would be so g-good if we were…" He paused. Now he was not only embarrassed but getting angry. This wasn't fair. He didn't embarrass her today in the cafeteria, or at least he tried not to. *She knows I so want to be with her. She's playing with me. If she doesn't want to see me, fine, but she shouldn't tease me this way.*

"You know what, Penny, I would love to talk to about your towel…and more but I think *that* is for two people who at least admit that they are interested in each other. " He felt a little better having at least temporarily recovered control of his tongue.

"Oh, Josh," she said, sounding a bit defensive and perhaps embarrassed herself. "We're friends; I was just flirting with you a little—"

"Look, Penny; I don't want to be just friends."

"Josh, I'm sorry. I really do think you're special. Um, well, let's just skip it; I apologize. I shouldn't have"—she sighed—"Look, it's like I've told you before…"

"Yeah, I know, you think I would disrupt your plan for college and everything else. Well love is not something that should stop a person from pursuing a dream; it should give him or her even more impetus to do what he or she… " He stopped in mid sentence. *Shit! He'd used the "L" word! How did that come out?* He could feel the familiar perspiration under his arms. His mind raced. Was that his mouth that formed those words? He did not mean for the "L" word to come out. I mean maybe he *felt* that way, in fact he *did* feel that way, but so what. A guy who was a senior in high school did not just *blindly blab* those words out, especially if he thought they were not going to be reciprocated. Now he was really embarrassed. *Wait—maybe she didn't pick up on it.* Silence.

"Josh," she said quietly and slowly. "What did you just say to me?"

Penny's floor may be wet by now, he thought, but suddenly he was the one feeling very naked here. "You know what, Penny; I don't even know. You made me mad and as so often is the case with you, I get flustered and who knows what comes out. Look, I've got homework and you're, uh, naked and I'm uh…hey…maybe I'll see you tomorrow." And with that he quickly put the phone in its cradle.

Holy shit, what have I done? he thought. *I need to make her think I'm moving on, not sound like a love-sick idiot.* If Sam knew he had done that, he would tie a sign around his neck with the word "asshole" on it and have a huge laugh, too! He sat on the bed in his parents' room for a while thinking about what he had said. The sad fact is he meant it. So there it was: Feeling those feelings with such intensity that your fingers actually hurt or you would swear you're having a heart attack. But you're supposed to be cool on the outside!

On the one hand, it actually felt good to say it. But on the other hand, he had opened up too much, considering their situation. He could hear his mother getting dinner ready in the kitchen and suddenly a little company and a different line of thought was an attractive alternative. He walked down the steps.

"What's for dinner tonight, mom?" He patted his mother on the shoulder. "Potato pancakes?"

Penny stood with the phone still in her hand, listening to the dial tone. She had nearly dried off already. She put the phone back on the cradle and sat on her bed. She suddenly felt cold and pulled the towel tighter around her. She noticed her door was open and she stood up and padded over to close it. She walked to her closet, dropped the towel, and pulled a Virginia Tech sweatshirt over her head. Not being comfortable with its length, she pulled on a pair of white panties. She sat on the bed, wondering what it would be like if Josh was there with her right now.

The implications of their conversation did not escape her. Even though he sort of hung up on her in anger, he was more than sort of hooked on her. She knew that it was not just because he got tongue tied at the thought of her with only a towel around her. But he had mentioned the "L" word and it hung there, like the little speech bubbles in a comic book. There had been total silence after that. What scared her was what he had said: That love should not get in the way of a person fulfilling his or her dreams. It was exactly how she felt, only *her* way of ensuring that was to deny its existence. *It's safer that way, isn't it?*

But why? She didn't have to live her mother's life or anyone else's life. She could have it all…couldn't she? Was this a crack in her armor? One thing she knew in her heart, whether she was ready to admit it or not, was that she wasn't yet ready to just let go of this boy who was certainly going to be a very good man someday soon. And if there actually was a boy anywhere on earth who would support her in pursuing her dreams, it might well be this one. But then there was the religious difference between them. This time of year really emphasized that! She lay on her bed thinking about Josh Gershwin for a long time.

It seemed as though the choice was hers. Finally, she reached over and turned off the light but she lay there in the dark for a while before falling asleep, her emotions swinging back and forth between feeling elated and being depressed.

CHAPTER XV
The Chapter Before Christmas

He had hardly talked to Penny much since the night the "L" word slipped out in their conversation on the phone. He had purposely avoided her in school whenever possible and during homeroom interludes, he busied himself talking to others. One day, though, as he had leaned down from his desk to pick up a pen that had rolled off, he found himself looking directly into her eyes as he swung back up into his seat again. There was a long pause as they had just sort of stared at each other for a moment. He finally broke the silence and said in a voice barely above a whisper, "When you blush, your face is even more beautiful than normal, which is really saying something." Then he spun forwards toward Mrs. Sutton at the front of the room, without waiting for a response from Penny or looking for any reaction.

He assumed there had been no response but as he briefly glanced at her, he saw that she was still looking at him. She was at a loss for words, he could tell. What a rare occasion! As he started to turn his head toward the front of the room she finally said, "Well thank you, but who said I'm blushing."

"Uh…I guess I did," he had said turning back towards her again. Before she could reply he said, "But, I could be wrong, you know, maybe the morning light just gives you a natural glow, you know?"

"You just can't stand it that now I know how strong your feelings are for me," she had whispered with her lips so close to his ear that he could feel her soft, warm breath. He quickly turned his face to her to respond and as he did, their lips were only inches apart. Penny drew back and before Josh could get a word out, Mrs. Sutton had caught sight of their antics and she bellowed, "Josh, I was going to make a few announcements before first bell but perhaps you or Penny have one or two you would like to share with us? The class would probably be more interested in what you two are discussing than anything I would have to say, I'm sure."

Of course the whole class had then swung around in their desks to face Josh and Penny with big smiles and nodding heads. Josh didn't care but he remembered seeing Penny absolutely horrified but Mrs. Sutton must have taken pity on her because at that moment she had corralled the class back in. Sharon was looking at her with an odd expression, which even Penny couldn't read.

"Never mind everyone, attention back up here. I don't have much time to go over the Christmas program schedule." That was the last time he had spoken to Penny, which was a week ago.

With only a few days before Christmas break, Josh decided two things. He was going to get Penny a present and he was going to figure a way to get her to go out with him on New Year's Eve. He was not giving up. First things first. He really had no idea what present he should get her. In a rare request for parental assistance, on any subject, but especially on a gift for someone, Josh decided to ask his mom for a few ideas on what he might give to a girl he was friends with. He happened to catch her by herself reading a magazine in bed one evening and decided to ask.

She took a deep breath and was about to shower him with a barrage of questions (which was why this was a "rare" event), when he blurted out, "She's cute, her name is Penny, no its not serious, and no she's not Jewish, she's Catholic. We're just friends." Caught with her breath fully inhaled and ready to speak, she let out a big sigh and she thought better of asking any (more) questions.

Still, he wasn't going to escape totally unscathed.

"You don't want it to be something too personal, Josh, since you are just friends. You are just friends, right Josh? That is what you said, right?"

Josh sighed, "Yes mother." He wished for once that he was lying.

She continued in the same breath, "...which is a good thing given that she is Catholic. Nothing against Catholics, Josh, you know that. Your dad and I both voted for Mr. Kennedy. It's just that one day, we want our grandchildren, to be Bar Mitzvah and be raised with all of the wonderful Jewish family traditions of our religion."

He naively replied, "There are wonderful family traditions in the Catholic religion, too, Mother." As if that was going to shift the discussion in his favor. She was not really listening any more but was looking in the J.C. Penny mail-order catalogue.

"What about a purse?" she dryly asked, flipping the pages.

He remembered Penny wearing the kind of small purse that looped around her wrist, which made it easy to hold while carrying books and walking to class. "That's a great idea. Done." His mom made him look through them all and pick several, saying if it was his gift to a friend then he should be the one to pick it out. She gave her approval to two of the ones he narrowed it down to and he made the final choice. He went to the department store after school the next day and found one just like it in the catalogue. He went straight to customer service and got it wrapped. He was glad that was over.

Now his thoughts turned to New Year's Eve. But as the holidays approached, he just wasn't sure how to approach this or even if he should. He felt he needed to do something to break up the log jam and make her see that there was something undeniable between them. A rare chemistry, that, rather than scaring her and making her run the other way, should draw her to him.

There were lots of New Year's parties being held to which he and Sam both had been invited, but he really didn't want to do that. He wanted to take her to dinner, just the two of them. No peer pressure, no loud music, and no typical teen antics. He also wanted to explain why he had needed her family information, his hunch, and what he had learned. But he wasn't going to just jump into that in a passing conversation as she might think it was some attention-getting ploy he thought up. That was more than a week ago. Time was getting short—just over a week left before December 31st that he began thinking of how he could make it happen. *I can do this!* he thought. *I can… but how?!*

He had tried his best to come up with a plan but finally admitted that maybe he needed some help. But from who? He thought about taking one or two of her best friends into his confidence but he quickly dropped that idea. He didn't have faith that they would keep it a secret nor that they would really help him pull it off. Besides, he halfway felt that Sharon was sending him all kinds of *"I'm available if she's not"* signals and Susan was too quiet and reserved to help him with devising a bold plan. Then it dawned on him. The most ridiculous idea he had ever had. So ridiculous, in fact, that he immediately dropped it. The trouble was it kept coming back to him and finally he decided, what the hell, he would try it.

He waited outside after the last day of school before the holidays, huddling against the wind, which, while not freezing, was chilly and damp. He identified her car, and sure enough as he looked up, Mrs. Sutton was approaching only a few yards away. She was dressed in a Christmas red long wool coat with black fur collar and black leather gloves, looking pretty spiffy as usual.

"Hi, Josh," she said as she looked for her keys in her purse. "Are you waiting for someone in this damp cold?"

"Uh yes, Mrs. Sutton, I'm waiting for you, actually." He nervously looked at his shoes.

"Well, here I am, Josh; what is it?" she answered in a surprisingly matter of fact way, as she pulled her car keys out of her purse.

"I wondered if I could talk to you about something and keep it just between us."

"Well, we can as long as you haven't killed any high-ranking Rebel officers or robbed any Confederate banks this week," she said with a bit of a smile.

He was quiet as he tried to figure out what to say. "You haven't done any of those things have you Josh?" she asked, opening the car door. "People don't take too kindly to you 'Blue Bellies' in these here parts, you know!"

She slid in and leaned across the seat to unlock the passenger door and motioned for him to get in. He hesitated for just a few seconds, but he realized that he had waited an hour for her and it was late, so he was unlikely to see anyone he knew at this point in the day. He quickly got in and closed the door. Out of the wind, it was immediately more comfortable and quiet. *Mrs. Sutton has good taste in cars,* he thought, as he felt the tan leather and took in the sporty look of a new navy blue Oldsmobile Cutlass. "Nice car, Ms. Sutton, this is the first year of the mid-size Cutlass," he observed, thankful for something to say.

"Well, thanks Josh, but I have to believe for you to risk being seen in a teacher's car by one of your cronies, you must have more on your mind. Let me guess, Josh. It has to do with one Penny Collingsly."

He stared at her in disbelief. "Holy sh….uh how did you know that? Am I wearing a tattoo on my forehead or something?"

"You may as well be, Josh. You kids are oblivious to other people's observations and perceptions in this school, but that doesn't mean they have none!" She tossed her purse in the back seat and rested her hand on the bottom of the steering wheel. "I've known for months that you were crazy about her, Josh. Aside from hearing the whispers and usual gossip after class and in the halls, it's very obvious the way you look at her. I also think that she feels very much the same way, but I can tell she is struggling with it a great deal. I assume that some of your antics this year have been because of your distraction with her, though I still wonder about that day you tried to replay Gettysburg in my homeroom!"

He sat silent, as if in the presence of the Amazing Carnac. The only thing missing was the envelope Johnny Carson would blow open and the great one's headdress! "Does that about sum it up, Josh?" She looked at him straight in the eye.

"You are amazing, Mrs. Sutton."

"Okay, I won't argue with that—now what is it you want from me?"

"Well, first, since you brought it up, there is an explanation for that day in your classroom where I led the charge against the Confederates but that's for another time. But I mention that because I don't want you to think I'm totally nuts."

"Alright, Josh, if you say so; but I'll reserve my opinion until I get the facts. Okay, back to Penny."

Josh tried to figure out the best way to approach this, but he finally just blurted it out. "I know some people would say, 'forget the whole thing; go to college next year and never look back.' I suppose I could do that but I don't want to. Why should I? I believe I am reasonably mature." Ms. Sutton was looking straight ahead and she smiled. "Well, most of the time anyway," he continued.

"Maybe even more than most guys my age, I don't know. I know what I want in life, though, and it begins with her. College and all of that yeah, but I want her sharing the experience with me, even if we are at different schools—I don't care. But she has this thing that she believes she'll have to give up her dream of going to college and having a profession if she gets into a relationship. I've tried to tell her that isn't the case at all—that I want her to do the things she wants to do but she is either scared or doesn't believe me, I guess. Maybe that happened to her mother, I don't know. We're….I'm still feeling my way along here. Mrs. Sutton, I just know I'm crazy about her even with the relatively little time we've actually been alone together. But I feel what I feel. Does that make any sense?"

He felt like a balloon that had just blown all its air out in one fell swoop.

"Yes actually, it does," she said softly. "Sometimes there's a chemistry that seems to be unleashed when two people are near one another. And it doesn't have to take long for it to be felt if it's for real. Hard to explain it."

He could see she was thinking of something, probably in her own past. He hadn't really planned on getting this deep into it with her, only to ask about how he might set up New Year's Eve, given the situation. But when it became obvious that she knew more than he thought she did, it just seemed natural to talk more about it with her.

They sat in silence for a few minutes. She looked at Josh and then said, "It sounds like you have made up your mind to continue to pursue this relationship. My feeling is it is almost always a mistake. It's usually a waste of your time. I never believe guys should push themselves at a girl for sex or for a relationship. That's because if the chemistry and feeling isn't there, all you get is a one-way road that ends in misery for all."

His demeanor visually sagged as he heard what she said and he started to protest but she hushed him with her finger to her lips.

"I said almost always a mistake, Josh. In your and Penny's case, I'm not so sure. From the little I've seen—and heard—I do believe there is a chemistry at work between you two, even if she hasn't fully admitted it to herself. And she sure isn't going to admit it to you before that revelation. You are right—and Lord knows I'll never again admit I said it—but I do believe you are a pretty mature young man, even if you do have your moments of, uh, adolescence!" She smiled at the rare admission she had just made to a student.

"Respectful persistence is okay. But with that comes the responsibility for knowing when you get an unmistakable signal from her to back off, and then all bets are off. However, I believe I know you well enough to know that your intentions are good," she said as she started the car. She looked over at Josh, which he took to be the signal that it was time to go and he pulled the door handle up. He was elated.

"Thank you Mrs. Sutton; I really do appreciate your help today." Then he paused after opening the door. "Just one more thing. I want to take her out on New Year's Eve—just the two of us—to a nice place for dinner. I just don't really know how to approach it with her without getting turned down."

"Did you get her a present for Christmas?"

"Yes, I got her one of those purses that she likes to wear around her wrist."

"Great choice, Josh! Are you sure you don't like older women?" she asked kidding. "Well, I would just take her the present on Christmas day and let the conversation develop naturally. Just be sure you have the plan set so you're not fumbling for what to do, where to go, et cetera. It's risky, but I would make your reservations in advance because that way you will know you can tell her where and what and when. She'll probably appreciate that you took the risk—that is, if she doesn't get mad at you for making too big an assumption so contrary to what she's been telling you." She laughed and shook her head. "It's all in how you explain it to her and approach it with her, Josh. Now I've got to get going, Mr. Gershwin."

But then she seemed to think of something and she paused. "Gershwin," she repeated. "Josh, aren't you Jewish? And isn't Penny Catholic?" She cocked an eyebrow at him. "Never mind. It makes it more complicated but you know that, I assume, and so does she. It may be another reason she is struggling."

Josh nodded and opened the door.

"I would never want to be seen as encouraging an interfaith relationship to any of my students, so I won't, Josh. Parents would kill me and rightfully so," she said as she looked straight ahead.

Josh got out of the car with a bit of a frown. "I understand, Mrs. Sutton. Thanks for letting me talk to you about this. You've been a big help." As he started to close the door Mrs. Sutton looked over at him with a smile and said, "Hey, but if it means anything, *I'm* Jewish and I married a wonderful Catholic man!" With that, Josh laughed and closed the door with a wave.

Mrs. Sutton pulled out from the curb with a slight squeal of the tires and waved goodbye to him with a grin.

Josh headed for home in better spirits than he had been for a long time. He felt that he had been validated. It was the right thing to do. He would definitely ask her for New Year's Eve—*New Year's Eve!*

CHAPTER XVI
Chestnuts Roasting

Christmas day dawned fair and warm with expected temperatures in the sixties, unusually warm for Richmond in December. Josh awoke and lay in bed knowing his parents were not going to be up early. It wasn't like it used to be when he was a kid and he got to take advantage of the Santa Claus thing. As a little boy he had really dug Santa and Christmas and his parents didn't want to break his heart with the truth. So they celebrated Chanukah as a religious celebration, and Christmas for fun. But those days were gone. No more Christmas celebrations in the Gershwin household, just a subdued Chanukah observance.

Josh stared at the ceiling, thinking about what Penny was doing right now. Was she still asleep or up with her family opening presents around a big warm fire and Christmas tree? He checked the clock: 9:35. Not too early for a Christmas morning. *Too warm out for a fire,* he thought. Had she given any more thought to his admission that he was in love with her? He would give her time to be with her family and then drop by unannounced to give her his present. At least, that was his plan for now. He kept vacillating back and forth between calling first or not. He wondered what was the right thing to do, given their current situation.

He was as ready as he could be for New Year's Eve. He had made reservations for two at Byrun's Restaurant on Broad Street for eight o'clock. At first, the woman on the phone said she didn't have anything open after five thirty, but after Josh explained to her the importance of this dinner date for his future, she laughed and said, "Well, I guess we can always find room for one more table."

Come to think of it, it didn't seem as funny to him as it did to her. But then again, how many times did she have some young guy try to explain to her that he was bringing his girlfriend there for dinner to convince her that she was actually his girlfriend? That was the part she seemed to find the funniest. Small wonder, he thought. He never would have brought it up except for the desperation he felt to try to convince her to find them a spot. *Never mind,* he thought. *Who cares? I've got the reservation. If Penny turns me down flat, I might have to send my parents so the reservation doesn't go unused.* A dismal thought, that. Actually his parents were not going to the club this year. They decided to just stay home and relax. His dad had been working crazy hours leading up to the holidays. That was fine with him. That meant the car was available.

He had more than enough money in the bank. He saved his money from working odd jobs for people in the neighborhood and during the summer at the golf club where his dad was a member. Dress was not a problem. Josh's dad was a buyer for a men's clothing store and he had always made sure Josh knew how to dress and that he had stylish suits and ties and such. Josh was actually more comfortable than most guys his age when it came to dressing for an event. He and Sam were a lot alike in that regard. So everything was set…with only one small detail to take care of: asking Penny to go!

Josh realized that he had been lying in bed for a long time now, doing all of this thinking and rehashing the past couple weeks. As he slid his legs to the side of the bed and put his feet on the floor, for some odd reason he thought about the rifle and wondered what kind of Christmases it had seen over its 100-plus year existence. Then remembering the inscribed date of 1862 on the silver plate, he realized that it was in fact 102 years old. He wondered in how many places had it greeted the morning of the birthday of Christ. He tried to change his thoughts to avoid encouraging the possibility of triggering another episode, but he couldn't help himself. Had it rested over a fireplace mounted on the wall of some cabin for years as the families knelt in front of the fire together on Christmas morning? Or had it been standing in the corner of some closet or attic for years, never seeing the daylight for Christmas or any other day?

Within minutes, and for the first time as if he had controlled it, the familiar dizziness came and he suddenly found his consciousness reawakening somewhere else in another time.

Only this time when he awakened, he was lying in a bed. He looked around and realized he was in a ward of what looked like some form of hospital, and definitely not a new one! As he tried to sit up, he felt a shooting pain in his head. A lot of pain. He felt something on his head and, quickly feeling around, he found it was a huge bandage wrapped completely around his skull. *What the hell was this?* he thought as he lay there, now feeling a dull ache in his forehead. He saw a woman dressed in white, and, assuming she was a nurse, he called out to her. "Miss uh …nurse… can you help me?" The nurse turned and looked at Josh as though she was seeing a ghost. Her eyes opened wide and her mouth jaw dropped. "My God!" she exclaimed as she came running to Josh's bed. "You're awake!" she said, eyes watering.

"I'm wondering what happened to me and where I…I am," Josh said. He tried to move his legs but the pain hit him again and he stopped.

"Son, you are in the Chimborazo hospital in Richmond. You've been here for a week," she said as she took his hand in hers. "We thought you were going to slip deeper and deeper into unconsciousness and finally just slip away from us altogether one day and that would be that."

"A week?" Josh asked in amazement. How could that be? He had just gotten here, hadn't he? Or at least he had just awakened here, having left the comforts of his room and soft, warm bed only moments ago. "I don't understand, I uh….just …well….seems like I just got here is all." He stammered, remembering he didn't want them to think he was delirious by telling the truth…or at least the truth as he knew it.

"Take it easy, son. You've been delirious, mostly unconscious now for a week. You got hit in the head with something, probably a rifle butt. You had a lump the size of a pine cone above the right side of your forehead. We kept it soaking in cool water compresses, so the swelling has gone down tremendously, but we weren't sure what was going on inside of that melon of yours. Your color is looking better, though, and your fever is broken," she said, feeling his forehead and patting his shoulder. "How are you feeling?"

"Well, I definitely got a headache, especially if I try to move, and I feel weak—other than that, alright, I guess." He realized that he felt exhausted. He looked at the nurse. She was probably in her late thirties, dark hair pulled back in a bun, no make up. Were there two of her? It was some double vision playing tricks on him. He wasn't sure what they called it back then, if anything, but he apparently had one hell of a concussion. He remembered nothing as to what had caused it. He was sure she must have seen many a rifle butt injury, so he took her at her words of experience.

She wore a white frock or smock or whatever such a covering was called that was too tight across her large breasts (he had no trouble seeing those). She had a full face, dark eyebrows, and pretty dark eyes with a straight narrow nose and medium thin lips. He also noticed that *he* was wearing only a white heavy cotton pullover nightgown that came down to his knees.

The nurse gave him a minute to get used to his surroundings as he quickly looked around. It went in and out of focus, but he could see that he was in some kind of ward with several other patients. He guessed it was a hundred feet long and twenty-five feet wide, just a rectangular box of a place with white wooden planks for walls and a ceiling; there was mostly natural light through the windows with gas lights, too.

"My name is Phoebe, Phoebe Pember, and I'm matron of this Chimborazo hospital." She motioned her hand in an arc. Josh did not like the looks of this place, nor did he savor its smell. He didn't like the sounds either. And it was hot. It was definitely not Christmas time here. He could hear moaning, coughing, and someone yelling in pain from somewhere. "Christ, I gotta get out of this place and now," he said out loud but not directing it at her in particular.

"What's your name, son?" she asked somewhat defensively.

"Josh Gershwin," he said a bit sheepishly. "I didn't mean to offend you," he said apologetically. "I'm just not used to this …uh… well, kind of place."

"Well, Josh Gershwin, let me tell you something. You're lucky you are in this hospital. If you'd been somewhere's else they probably *would've* tossed you in a corner and let your fever build until you either died from the fever or just became a mute or an idiot for life. Especially if they had had dozens of boys piled up in the hallways or outside of a tent hospital, bleeding and screaming with more coming in every minute from the battle front. Not to mention, you're a Yankee! You are in what is probably the largest military hospital in the world, young Josh, and if you hadn't noticed, we are of the Confederate persuasion. There are some eighty wards exactly like this one on forty acres, Josh. We've got 3,000 patients, all soldiers wounded or sick or both."

"Are you serious?" he asked in amazement.

She looked at him, wondering why he would ask her if she was serious. He realized that some of his colloquialisms might not be understood in this time period.

"Yes, I'm serious Josh. We're high on a bluff in the westernmost end of Richmond."

He had a million questions about what had happened to him and how he got there, and more, but he was feeling fatigued and his head was throbbing. He touched the bandage that wrapped his head. "Was I cut bad, too?" he asked, pushing only gently against the bandage and getting the obvious response…pain.

"No, just a slight tear. It must have been the flat side of the butt that hit you, which is why instead of getting a bad cut you got knocked out for so long. The force of the blow might have killed someone with, uh, more stuff in his head." She smiled with that and Josh couldn't help but smile, too.

"You mean like someone who had more brains?" He then laughed and then winced because it made his head hurt more.

He noticed that she was wearing a thin necklace that had a small silver Star of David pendant on it. *That might come in handy*, he thought, as he filed it away for future reference. Getting back to her obviously prideful description of the hospital, she said, "And we're adjacent to the Oakwood Cemetery, too."

"Oh, well, isn't that convenient at least," he said with a smirk, looking directly at her. She tried to stifle another smile. "You know I really appreciate your taking care of me, but if you could just bring me my, uh, 'navy blues' and maybe scrounge up a cane somewhere, I think I'll just be on my way."

This time she laughed out loud. She believed this young man, based on his looks and his sense of humor, to probably be Jewish (not to mention that she had noticed in taking care of him while he was unconscious that he was circumcised, which, unlike today, was still relatively confined as an everyday occurrence to Jewish boys in the mid-nineteenth century). He seemed an odd mixture of boy and man—quite a catch for some young woman. Definitely a product of good upbringing and well educated, to boot. She could tell he wasn't even aware of the special circumstances of his being wounded and captured.

Fixing her dark eyes on him and getting serious again she said, "Even if you were well enough to walk, I can't just let you go. Most patients here are Confederates, of course, but not all. Some are like you, wounded Union soldiers awaiting death or recovery. When you recover, they typically ship you off to a prison stockade or camp." Then lowering her voice to a whisper she said, "But you're safer here with the remnants of a huge knot on your head than you are in one of those camps with no wound at all, as I hear it told. Lots of captured prisoners sick and dying in those camps." She wouldn't tell *him* yet but she was going to try to find a way to prevent that, if possible.

She looked left and right to make sure no one had heard her talking about the poor conditions of their prisoner camps. The soldiers in the bed on either side of Josh were both asleep, or in a coma—he couldn't tell—and he didn't want to know. He didn't look too close. He was suddenly very aware that he was a Union soldier in a

Confederate hospital. That alone was a scary thought. What an irony: He's in his own hometown, some one hundred years removed, but he's a Union soldier. Why the hell was he not a Confederate in these damn flashbacks? Why had he thought about that stupid rifle, anyway? Just asking for trouble, like an idiot.

He just prayed he would wake up soon and be out of this. He sure as hell wasn't going to some place like Andersonville in South Carolina, which he had studied in school with its infamous death toll during the Civil War. He still had no clue if these episodes were real in any way. Was he vulnerable to a wound or illness? He put his hand on his forehead where the bandage was. It was swollen and warm. Not since he had banged his head in one of his earliest flashbacks had he felt any pain associated with these episodes and nothing like an actual wound.

He was feeling fatigued and Phoebe Pember could see he needed to sleep. She moved in the direction of one of the beds next to him. "Josh, you get some sleep. I think you're going to be much improved over the next couple of days." She lowered her voice to a whisper. "I can't let you go anywhere just yet, but we may be able to figure out something when you get your strength back. I don't want to see you shipped off to one of those godforsaken camps either. I didn't feed you, bathe you, and nurse you through this mess to do that."

His face turned red as he thought about being bathed, remembering he only had on a short night gown. And what about the bathroom? He for sure wasn't going to delve into that little bit of history, at least not until he had to "go." He was convinced he could walk if he had to. "Besides," she said, "I can't let a fellow Hebrew and a hero, even if you are on the other side, get sent to one of those places."

"Hebrew hero?" he mumbled. He had a lot of cobwebs in his head and was drifting off to sleep. "We'll talk later," she said as she turned to leave his bed. He was already asleep.

CHAPTER XVII
Grabbed

Charles Parcel Junior's letter to his family back home in western Virginia said that through an odd but peaceful meeting, he and a young Union soldier by the name of Josh had talked about home and the long war and that he had made up his mind then and there that he was going back home, desertion or not. He realized that he did not want to kill this young man, who was so much like himself. He just couldn't see any sense in the fighting and he didn't believe in the South's wanting to break up the Union anyhow.

They shook hands and wished each other well, he wrote, and Charles had made his way along the banks of the Bull Run stream, trying to distance himself as much as possible from all the troops there under the cover of dusk. He walked for several hours that hot August night but was exhausted from the previous day's marching and action and finally laid down in the woods and fell asleep. He stated, *"I woke that first dawn of my new freedom as the sun's light just peaked through the woods. I ate the rest of the salt pork I had in my haversack. I wasn't gonna wear that Confederate uniform no more so I tossed the jacket and the hat and* put on a straw hat I found near a farm and tossed them "uncom'table" boots too. So now I was barefoot, with my favorite short sleeve tan shirt, my old brown pants and my new straw hat. Nobody would mistake me for a Reb anymore."

He decided he would walk at night to keep from being seen for fear of being accosted by soldiers of either side. So he'd quit walking at dawn and find a place to sleep. Then he'd wake up in late afternoon or early evening. To pass some of the long hours he decided to keep a journal of his adventures on the long walk home since he had his Bible with extra pages and a pencil. He'd write for an hour or two, just before it got dark, and then get back on the trail using the sunset and the moon as his guides to head west toward home.

According to his journal, Charles, after two days, was starving. There was water enough as he found lots of streams, which was a good thing because he had tossed his canteen with his other equipment. He had a knife but that wasn't doing him much good. He was a decent rifle hunter, but of course the rifle was gone as well; he tossed it to avoid looking suspicious. Knives were a different thing altogether. The streams were too narrow and shallow for fishing, even if he could improvise a pole and hook. He finally had to take a chance so he stopped at a farmhouse where he saw a woman working near the barn. He asked her if he could work the day for some food. She said with her husband gone a year to fight in General Lee's army, she could use some help. He spent two days cutting firewood and sharpening knives, axes, and such. It was worth it. She gave him a gunny sack with apples, carrots, a metal cup, salted pork, and even a decent pair of weathered shoes and old knitted socks for his poor sore feet.

The food would hold him for a week if he conserved it carefully. As best he could tell, he was about a week into his journey with a long way to go. He'd come about 140 miles in that week, based on the farm lady's estimate of how far she lived from Manassas. He began to take less precautions as time wore on. He started walking more in the morning to noon or so and sleeping more at night. He could make better time that way during the day. Then suddenly, one morning while he was sitting on a big log taking a breather, he felt something pointed shoved against his back.

"Don't move or I'll put a bullet right where you feel this here barrel in the middle of your back. Walk two steps forward and turn around slowly." Charles did what he was told and turned around to see that he was facing a Union soldier with some fifteen or twenty others behind him on horseback. He was probably in his early twenties, with blond hair and blue eyes, but he had the look of an older, more experienced man. One who had seen much killing and dying, no doubt.

"Alright boy, who are you and what are you doing slinking around these woods?"

"Sir, I was a Confederate soldier but I done had enough of this here war and I'm headed home to West Virginia to my family's farm," Charles said, figuring it best to just tell the truth.

"Well boy, you know, a Reb without his uniform is nothing but a damned spy is all. We hang spies, you know that?" The corporal turned back towards his patrol and hollered to the sergeant. "Hey sarge, I think we got us a Reb spy here. I say we hang him right here and not waste time dragging him back to camp." Turning back to Charles with breath that would peel paint from a barn, he said, "We're out here to find all you damn sissies, deserters, and spies from both sides of these armies and make examples of yer kind."

With that he reached over and grabbed Charles by the arm and jerked him toward the patrol. At that moment, the sergeant trotted his horse forward and said "Private Tolson, tie his hands and put him behind you on your horse. We ain't hanging nobody out here. Who do you think you are, a damned hanging judge? Our orders are to bring in the stragglers and that's what we're gonna do. Confederate or Union, don't matter till we get 'em to camp. If they believe he's a spy, they'll try him and hang him if they say he's guilty."

As Charles' journal recounts, for two days they rode and camped at night. On the second day, he found himself in a base camp not far from Richmond where a portion of a Union supply train was stationed. He was lead to a big, dirty gray tent with about twenty other soldiers. A few were in blue, some in Confederate butternut or grey and some like him with old farm clothes on.

The rumor was that each "prisoner" not dressed in uniform would get a chance to tell his story to a court marshal of sorts there in the camp and a decision would be made on what to do with him. Charles was fearful of either being shot or hanged as a spy or sent to some prison camp up north as a captured Confederate soldier. None of these was acceptable in his mind. He had to get out of here somehow.

He looked around the tent and suddenly he noticed a young Union soldier sitting on the other side of the tent that looked familiar. His journal described it this way. *"I see this feller sitting up against one of the tent poles, his dirty brownish Reb uniform looking much too small for him. It was without a doubt the same UNION soldier I had made friends with at Manassas. Josh was his name. By God, they got us both! Why was he wearing a Reb uniform? Hell, they must have gotten Josh for spying too. Either that or they just figured he was another Reb soldier since he was in a Confederate uniform. He might be in as much danger as me unless he's got a damn good explanation."* Spies and deserters were made examples of in the worst way, or so he'd been told by friendly Private Tolson. Charles began to slowly edge his way between the others sitting on the ground in the tent until he was next to Josh, who hadn't noticed his movements.

"*Josh,*" he whispered so as not to be heard by the guards posted at the tent's doorway. Most of the other prisoners were either sleeping or talking amongst themselves. There was no discernable difference between the Confederate and Union prisoners at this point.

CHAPTER XVIII
The Promise

Josh, upon hearing his name, turned quickly toward the voice and immediately recognized Charles. Not that he was focusing on it, but this was the first time he had met the same person in two different flashbacks. *Was that significant? Hell, who knows.* He hadn't made the acquaintance of too many people in these flashbacks anyway. They shook hands, exchanged hellos, and immediately got down to discussing how they had gotten into this mess and how they were going to get out of it.

Josh explained to Charles that he had awakened in the hospital in Richmond with no memory of how he was injured. As he had now found out that Charles had only been gone less than two weeks, Josh knew he had to have been injured literally around the same time Charles left, since he knew he had been in the hospital a week. He told Charles how the young, pretty nurse had cared for him and got him a Reb uniform that he could put on to escape. She said she hadn't saved his life only to see him shipped to some butcher pen of a prison camp.

She also told him that rumor had it that the events of his being wounded and captured were the result of his trying to keep a fellow Union soldier from going after a young Rebel he saw making his way into the woods when the day's fighting had ended. Josh, according to the young nurse's story, had apparently been hit in the head by a rifle butt as he tried to prevent the soldier from running after the disappearing Reb. He was left for dead and was later discovered by Rebel special details crossing the battlefield that evening, looking for the wounded among the many bodies strewn across the fields near the old McLean farm at Manassas. Josh remembered that he had heard an angry voice before drifting out of that flashback. Was it literally part of some action that continued? Who knew?

"That means you done saved my neck, you damn fool," Charles said with a trace of a smile and sincere gratitude. "I bet that damn blue belly…uh no offense meant, Josh….was going to follow me and shoot me right in the back for his trophy!"

"Well, regardless, I got out of that damn hospital thanks to Miss Pember and her stolen little Reb uniform two sizes too small for me. You should have seen her, Charles, she didn't even sneak me out. She brought me the uniform during the night and told me to just get out of bed in the morning and put it on and wait. I did just that, feeling a little woozy in the head, and she walked into this room full of wounded soldiers, took my arm, and guided me down the hall and out of the building as if I was just the best *Johnny Reb* you've ever seen. She gave me a hug and said loudly with a wink, that '*I should get going and find my unit in Richmond.*' That was that. They all thought I was a Reb for sure.

"Then I had to figure out what to do next, as I had no clue where I was supposed to be." Josh could have said that he prayed then as he did now, that the flashback would end with him back in his home safe and sound, but Charles would think he was mad. They both sat silent, Charles waiting for Josh to continue and Josh just thinking about those past few days.

In the midst of the stupid flashback, he had had no idea where to go after leaving the hospital. Where does a kid from 1964 Richmond, Virginia, go when he finds himself wandering around in *1862* Richmond, Virginia? If he hadn't been so scared, it would have been an incredible adventure as he wandered around the east end of Richmond down near Churchill and the James River. He noticed that St. John's Church, where Patrick Henry's *"give me liberty or give me death"* speech was made prior to the American Revolution, looked worse in the 1860s than in the future. He had found Richmond to be dirty and filled with noisy smoky bars, prostitutes, wild soldiers, and such.

On the streets, lots of strange smells—some good and some bad—assaulted his nose. He noticed, except for the sound of horse hooves and carriage wheels clacketing on many cobblestone streets, that it was quiet.—much quieter than he was used to, with the taken for granted sounds of buses, cars, industry, airplanes, and other noises of modernity. The other thing that he noticed quickly was how small everything was and cramped. The houses and buildings were so small and crowded together that Richmond appeared like one of those little towns you pass through in the deep South, even in 1964. It was not too friendly a place for a young man not experienced in the ways of the street.

Charles sat quietly, studying his new friend trying to put his finger on why this just seemed so odd. He gave up though and looked to Josh for him to continue the story.

"Well, it's a short story, my friend," Josh continued finally. "Thinking I could walk around like I owned the place, blending in with my Reb uniform, I just headed out on a dusty well-traveled road, but after several miles of twists and turns and other dirt roads crisscrossing it, I got lost and the next thing I knew, I had wandered into an area of just fields and woods. Suddenly I found myself face to face with a Union supply sergeant. He quickly grabbed his pistol and here I am. A Union patrol picked me up near his supply train. I can't prove I'm Union because I have no unit to go back to." Charles started to speak but Josh interrupted him. "Don't even ask; it's a long story. Just take my word for it."

Charles looked around quickly and said softly, "Well, we got to get ourselves out of this camp and on to the next phase, which for me is home and for you…well, I won't pry but seems like you must have some kind a place you got to go to. Any ideas on what to do?"

"Yes," Josh quickly whispered, "I was thinking about it before you came in and night is for sure the best time. The guards don't really care about staying awake all night long to guard what they think are a bunch of misfits, which come to think of it is a pretty good description of you and me and maybe most of these guys.

"I think if we can stay alert, sneak out of the tent without waking anyone inside and not waking the guard at the door, we can sort of melt into the woods. If anyone asked what you're doing, just say you're taking a whiz."

"Uh, okay, Charles stammered. "Uh, what's a whiz?"

Shit, Josh had slipped back into his native tongue. "Oh, that's a folksy term from my family for relieving yourself in the woods, you know."

"Ah, got it. Alright, I'm with you; let's just try and stay unnoticed and out of trouble till dark."

That was easy enough. No one in the tent was doing anything but playing cards or sleeping. They waited for the guard to change after dark, figuring the relief guard would be on duty all night and would probably fall asleep before too long. To Charles' misery, the guard was Tolson, the same soldier who had threatened him when he was taken prisoner and he immediately began intimidating the whole group.

"Alright you bastards, no card playing and no talking. I don't want to see you all bunched up anywhere you spread it out. Nobody closer than a yard or more to each other." Then even in the dim light he recognized Charles.

"Hey, you little bastard, I remember you from earlier today. I would a-hung you for sure if the sergeant hadn't a-stopped me. You're a poor excuse for a solider, that's for sure. Where you from, boy?"

Charles didn't answer. The soldier got up and walked over to where Charles was sitting on the ground and kicked him in the side, hard. With the wind knocked out of him, he could barely breathe, let alone talk. He managed to wheeze, "southwest Virginia!"

"Ain't nobody worth a damn living in those hills and mountains back there. No wonder you're worthless." Charles was ready to spring up and hit this son of a bitch, but his side was still hurting and Josh was shaking his head and motioning for him to stay put.

The soldier noticed Charles trying to read Josh's meaning and walked over to Josh. "What are you up to? Are you trying to send that boy some signals? Like maybe the two of you trying to jump me or somethin'?" Even standing over Josh from two feet away, his smell washed over him, like when he used to walk through the dairy exhibit at the state fair in Richmond. *My God, how could he even stand himself,* Josh thought as the smell of ten different things, all bad, mixed together and nearly made him sick.

Charles knew exactly what that look on Josh's face was and couldn't resist. "Hell, we wouldn't want to get close enough to you to jump you. You smell like you slept in the privy."

With that, the soldier spun around raised his rifle and pointed the bayonet directly at Charles' throat. "Why, you little West Virginia skunk, I'm gonna put this bayonet through your throat and then we'll see how much talkin' you do." He pulled the rifle back with a snapping movement like he had been taught, but at the exact moment before he could lunge toward Charles, Josh rolled right into his legs from behind, buckling his knees and sending him flying backwards. He fell over Josh, then quickly grabbed his rifle and stood up fuming, putting his focus now on Josh, who had made him look foolish. "You're a dead man", he said, stepping back from Josh and putting the long rifle musket up to his shoulder to aim.

By now, the rest of the gang in the tent was tired of listening to him bully everyone, especially the two young men. As he cocked the flintlock, one of the prisoners who must have been six foot six, the biggest man in the tent, with a massive head full of dark long hair, grabbed him from behind, spun him around, and put a knee in his groin. As he doubled over in pain, the large man dressed in a combination of blue pants and grey shirt clasped his hands together and brought them down on the poor man's neck. *Smack!* With a slight whimper, he dropped to the ground in a heap with his rifle noisily clanging to the dirt.

Without saying a word, the large man reached down, picked up the rifle and the unconscious guard like he was a sack of potatoes, and carried him to the entrance of the tent, where he put him in the chair, arranged him nicely, and laid his rifle across his lap. To all the world he appeared to be doing what the rest of the guards were usually doing, sleeping.

The big guy just winked at Josh and Charles and went back to his place and lay down, putting his floppy hat over his face. All was quiet again and Josh and Charles did not have to worry about waking the guard anymore!

Three hours later, they stood in the woods with the camp fires from the place they'd just left barely visible. "You know, you could have got yourself killed back there trying to keep that idiot from sticking me," Charles said. "I won't forget that. That's the second time you saved me. The first time got you laid up in a hospital with your head nearly crushed. I'm gonna be obliged to you forever, you know that? I don't know how, but some day, I'm gonna repay you, Josh, I promise."

As they parted company, Josh watched Charles make his way into the dark woods. He could hear his feet snapping twigs when he could see him no more. Then he was gone.

Josh walked for an hour with the light from the quarter of a moon. There was just enough light to see a little, which kept him from running into the trees, though the occasional stump or raised root would send him stumbling to regain his balance. He really had no idea where he was going. He suddenly realized that with all the commotion he had not mentioned Penny to Charles. Then he thought, *how on earth would I have explained that little scenario. Oh yes, Charles, I know your future great great granddaughter!* At last he felt it was safe to lie down and get some sleep. As he closed his eyes, he heard Charles' last words echoing in his head, *I'm gonna repay you, I promise!*

CHAPTER XIX
The Christmas Card

The sound of music woke Josh in the bright morning light. Fearing it might be some evangelist coming through the woods, Josh slowly opened his eyes and quickly saw the radio on his nightstand, awash in morning sunlight, and heard the soft strands of "O Come, All Ye Faithful."

"Oh thank God I'm back," he said. He sat up quickly, relieved to be in his own room and bed once again. He had almost gotten used to these crazy events. He looked at the clock; it was only a few minutes later than it had been before his "journey." This one was particularly vivid, as he recalled what had happened and where he'd been. *Christ, I feel as though I'd been gone for a month.* Then he remembered that it was Christmas Day. Sometimes he could remember exactly what happened in the flashbacks but not always. It was almost like a dream. *Maybe that is all it really was, a recurring dream.* Except a couple of times he had been wide awake when they occurred, which was not one's typical daydream.

He had seen Charles again. He also had been injured and in the hospital. His head had been bashed pretty good. *Well, sometimes people get hurt in their dreams but it doesn't mean anything; they're fine when they awake.* With that he sprang out of bed, went quickly to the bathroom, and, pushing the dark locks out of his eyes, checked to see if he had any telltale signs like a bruise, swelling, or pain. As a matter of fact, he did have a discoloration on his forehead: a small area near his hairline that was almost purplish, like a bruise that is going away. A wave of goose bumps came over him. He touched it and did not feel any pain. *A coincidence again? Who knows.* Suddenly he realized that his bladder was sending him a signal that it would soon burst if he didn't take action. As he stood there in his cotton briefs, his mind returned to his main focus, Penny; but something nagged at him about his latest journey back through time. He kept thinking that there was something important he should remember, but his mind was in sort of a fog. The thought of Penny made him anxious. He missed seeing her and talking with her. He was either going to rekindle her feelings for him or make a fool of himself trying. His confidence was shot, though. Did she still have feelings for him? Yes, absolutely….well…he thought so, anyway. Today would tell.

    He took her present out of the closet with the card he had bought her. *I hope she's going like this purse,* he thought. He reread the card to make sure it sounded right. That's how he was going to spring the surprise on her for New Year's Eve…in the card. It was okay—a serious card for a serious holiday and a very serious situation, in his mind. Maybe not to some, but for him this was a crossroads. He also prided himself on his sense of humor, so he had tried to keep the card light; and of course, never show fear!

    Aside from the usual best wishes for a Merry Christmas and Happy New Year, he had neatly pasted inside, a card he had typed for the occasion. It read:

*Should auld acquaintance be forgot and never
brought to mind
Please dine with me on Thursday next, as we
toast to auld lang syne*

A reservation has been made for Ms. Collingsly and a certain Mr. Gershwin to dine at Byrun's Restaurant, one of the finest culinary establishments in Richmond, on New Year's Eve, December 31, 1964, at 8:00 p.m.

Yours truly, Josh

After much consternation he had finally decided to sign the card, *Yours Truly*, which, while pretty common, said almost what he wanted to say since he thought signing it "Love, Josh" might be too aggressive at this point in their "relationship."

Josh took his time getting showered and dressed and put on his best casual clothes: a long sleeve Gant oxford cloth light blue cotton shirt with the button-down collar and lots of starch, so it looked perfect. He also donned a pair of navy blue bell-bottom pants with his best Nettleton cordovan colored boots. His favorite cologne, Canoe, rounded out the preparation.

His mom was sitting at the breakfast table, reading the paper, and his dad was watching an old movie, both having eaten breakfast while he was getting dressed. "Good morning, Josh," his mother said. "Are you hungry?"

"Good morning, mother; Merry Christmas to all. I need to ride over to Penny's to give her the present, uh, I got her. The purse, remember?"

"I do, yes ,Josh, now that you mention it. Don't you want something to eat first?" *Mothers are always trying to feed you—especially Jewish mothers,* Josh noted to himself.

"No thanks, not hungry this morning."

"Don't be home too late; we're having a big dinner around four thirty." She saw his questioning look. "Well, its Christmas, for Christ's sake", she said with a smile.

"Hmmm, okay to celebrate it to eat but not to give presents? I guess we gotta eat regardless, so that's fine. Hey, dad, if you change your mind about giving me a Christmas present, I'll take a little Jaguar XKE."

"Ok, Josh, I'll remember that. Too bad you didn't tell me that a couple weeks back. I really struggled with what to get you for Chanukah."

"Well, I haven't worn the sweaters yet; is it too late to return them?"

"Funny, Josh, very funny."

Josh got his keys and Penny's present with the card and headed out the door. The weatherman had been exactly right. Sixty degrees with a light cloud covering. It still looked like a typical winter and Christmas day; it was just a bit warm, that's all.

Brushes enjoyed the respite from chilly temperatures and came up to greet Josh as he came down the step from the front porch. "Hi, boy. Merry Christmas to you, Brushes. Hey, are you Jewish, Brushes? I hope so for your sake, since you don't get a Christmas either. Hmmm, come to think of it, you don't want to be. You'd have to be circumcised, and at this point in your life, I doubt it would be worth it."

As usual, Brushes listened intently to his young master but reserved his comments out of respect, no doubt.

The drive to Penny's was long and unnerving. At first Josh couldn't wait to get there and then the closer he got, the more he worried about what her reaction was going to be. When he was rounding the curve past the Baird Park reservoir, he almost got cold feet. He circled around through the park several times before finally deciding to go for it. It was after half past eleven in the morning by now. As he pulled up to her house, the first thing he noticed was that her family car was not out in front. He parked and got out of the car and walked slowly toward the front door, looking for any sign that someone was home. He tried to tell himself it was too bright out to see any lights, but with the overcast skies he could see through the windows that it was dark inside. Before he even rang the bell, he was sure that there was no one home. What if they were out of town for the day? What if they were out of town for the whole Christmas vacation? They could easily have gone to see family. *What a jerk I am,* he thought. *I should have forgone the surprise.*

He rang the doorbell listlessly, knowing there would be no answer. As he turned to leave, he was shocked to hear the door open. He turned quickly again and found himself face to face with Penny.

"Hi, Josh," she said with what he wanted to believe was a mixture of surprise and real pleasure, even relief. Or was that just wishful thinking? "Happy Holidays to you," she said. She was still in her bathrobe and pajamas and looked exactly as he thought she would—in a word, beautiful. She wore just a touch of makeup, probably from yesterday. Her dark hair was a little tossed but the natural curls against her sculptured cheekbones made him remember how sweet her hair smelled the night at Sam's party when they danced.

"Merry Christmas, Penny. I thought for sure there was no one home."

"Are you disappointed then?" she asked jokingly.

"Uh, n-n-no, absolutely not." He surprised himself with his nervousness.

"My parents went to church this morning and then to my mom's best friend's house for a brunch. I did not feel like going for some reason. I sort of like to stay home on Christmas morning."

"To contemplate your presents?" Josh asked.

"Hmm, sometimes. Are you one of my presents this morning, Josh?"

"Well, no I…I mean yes….I mean…here's a little something I bought for you." He could feel the familiar moisture under his arms. Jesus, she had such an effect on him. Was she teasing him nicely or taunting him?

She took the present and the card. He was glad it was wrapped nicely.

"Why don't you come in, Josh?" she asked as she opened the door for him and stepped back.

"Thanks," he said, as he stepped up and into the house. It immediately smelled like her and was much like he imagined. He saw light, bright colors. The living room was small but nicely furnished with comfortable pastel yellow and green sofas and Danish modern furniture.

"I should go and get dressed," she said, starting to turn.

"Don't feel you have to get clothes on for me," he said and then quickly added, "I mean you are fully dressed, really."

She sat down on the larger sofa and motioned for him to do the same.

"You didn't have to do this, Josh," she said as she set down the gift and started to open the card.

"I know it's typical to open the card first but in this case I'd like you to do it last, if that's okay."

"Sure," she said as she switched the items and began opening the gift wrap on the box. As she opened the box and took out the purse, she was truly touched. "Josh, this is so beautiful. You could not have gotten me anything better. You really noticed what I like, didn't you?"

"Well, I tried to. I'm glad you like it. I saw it and it said that it was for you."

"Can I open the card now?" she asked, reaching for it.

"Uh, yes, you… that…I mean yes, you should do," he then sighed, exasperated with himself. "Yes."

She smiled at him. As she opened the card, he watched her eyes as she read the little phrase and then saw her eye catch the card in the center of the page. She read it and then he could see she read it again and again. Was she stalling for a way to let him down easy so as to minimize the hurt to him on Christmas Day?

"I don't know what to say, Josh," she said finally, looking at him, her face coloring slightly. "I have plans for New Year's Eve already."

He smiled through his anguish. "It's okay; I knew it was probably too late. I wanted to ask you sooner, but, uh…well….it was hard because you weren't…uh…I mean I wasn't able…" He paused, feeling silence was better. The worst part was she was going to be with someone else. He felt a pain deep in his chest.

"Yeah," she sighed, "I was planning to just sort of watch old movies on TV and see the midnight network celebrations. But you know, I think maybe those plans are flexible, Mr. Gershwin." She looked directly into his eyes.

"Does that mean you will go with me?" he asked, trying hard not to sound like a little schoolyard idiot.

She nodded, still looking directly into his eyes. Her almond-shaped eyes simply melted him. "Josh, this has been the nicest Christmas anyone could have given me. I know I've been standoffish…hmm, maybe that's not quite strong enough," she said, reacting to his long blink. "You know my reasons and I still have a few reservations but, if you are willing to take your chances knowing that, then I'd like to go with you New Year's Eve."

It was all he could have hoped for. He just wanted a chance to show her that she had no reason to fear that he would cast a shadow over her independence or her dreams. And the Jewish-Catholic thing would just be a bump they could overcome. But one thing at a time.

"Well, I better get myself dressed before my parents come home. They aren't used to seeing boys here with me in my jammies," she said as she stood up. Her robe slightly parted open, revealing silk blue pajamas. "Actually neither am I, but you make me feel so damn comfortable, Josh. Is that a weapon you have?" She extended her arms and pulled him up from the sofa when he took her hands.

"Well, I wouldn't call it a weapon. In fact, you know they say nice guys finish last."

Still holding his hands, she leaned in and kissed him softly on the mouth. Taking a step backwards, she looked at him and said, "Sometimes it's just finishing that counts…and sometimes finishing last is best." And with that, she smiled and wrapped her arms around him. They kissed for a long time.

EPILOGUE

On June 10th 1968, Penny Collingsly graduated *magna cum laude* from the University of Virginia with a pre-law degree. That same June, Josh Gershwin graduated with honors from Virginia Tech with a degree in communications.

Also in that same month, Penny and Josh were married in a dual ceremony by a Reform Rabbi and a Catholic priest, with Sam as Best Man and Sharon as Maid of Honor. Their parents were present, and though less than ecstatic about the mixed religious implications, all were convinced that God could see these two young people were very much in love. Their wedding vows were a combination of the traditional Jewish and Catholic ceremonies, with a special vow written by Josh, which he recited at the end of the ceremony.

"Only one person in the world fills my days with happiness from morning till night. There is only one person with whom I want to spend my whole life and who will be the mother of our children. That is my new wife, Penny. No words ever sounded sweeter. There is one special person whom I owe for making this all possible. He made me a promise once that

he would find a way to repay me for a good deed. His name was Charles and he more than made his promise come true."

He looked at Penny and she winked at him, acknowledging her full recollection of his accounting to her of his flashbacks and her understanding of who Charles was if not exactly how he had woven his spell over them.

And with that, as per the traditional Jewish wedding custom, Josh stomped the glass in the napkin and he kissed Penny for a long time.

And as fate would have it, for some strange reason, the flashback where Josh and Charles bid farewell was the last flashback that Josh ever had.

ACKNOWLEDGEMENTS

The Civil War scenes in this book are a product of many years of reading about the war, viewing great films and attending the 125th and 135th re-enactments of the battle of Gettysburg. However, I would like to acknowledge a few specific sources of special inspiration.

Of Gods and Generals by Jeff Shaara, Ballantine Books New York copyright 1996 , The Visual Dictionary of the Civl War by John Stanchak A Dorling Kindersley Book copyright 2000, Jewish Women's Archive. "JWA - Nurses - Phoebe Yates Levy Pember", www.jwa.org/discover/inthepast/infocus/military/nurses/pember.html> (April 2, 2006), To The Gates of Richmond- Stephen W. Sears Houghton Mifflin Co.

Printed in the United States
201810BV00002B/316-366/P